Neither Night nor Day

Neither Night nor Day

Written and Illustrated
by
Meryl Dowman

Published by

Vajra Books
Kathmandu

Vajra Publications
Kathmandu, Nepal

Distribution:
Vajra Book Shop
PO Box 21779, Kathmandu, Nepal
http://www.vajrabooks.com.np
Tel/fax: 977-1-4220562

ISBN 978-9937-506-16-8

Printed in Nepal

For Ariane, Jason and Keith with love

Where the mountain streams run ice-cold through the barley fields and the high plateau meets an azure sky, there lived a boy called Jigme. He was not so old, nor was he still very little, but he had yet to find out if he could live up to his name – which means fearless.

One early summer morning he sat on his doorstep watching the clouds like long curls of dragon's breath drifting across the sky. Little Leo his dog was sitting next to him, lifting his shaggy ears from time to time at the sounds of distant dogs barking on the hillside. It was a beautiful day but Jigme was sad and distracted. His mother had not been well for some time. Her eyes had lost their usual sparkle and even when she did smile it seemed to make her tired. None of the medicine she took appeared to be doing her any good and the boy was worried about her.

But as he sat there, he felt there was something promising in the air. It was such a fair and sunny day and a warm teasing wind running from the south was rejoicing in the season's change. High above the rooftops a wisp of cloud separated itself off in fine silky strands and unravelled into the blue. For a moment it resembled an outstretched arm and a beckoning finger before it dissolved and vanished altogether. Jigme came to a decision and stood up. If no one in the local villages could cure his mother's illness he would set out and find someone somewhere else who could.

His father was away on business. His elder brothers and sisters were out in the high pastures herding the yaks and sheep. There was only one person around who could give him advice and that was his great-uncle Rabten.

He left his house and went off into the village to look for him. It did not take long. Great-uncle Rabten was standing in the middle of the main street examining the toes of his felt boots with great concentration.

"Please, uncle Rabten, can you help me?" Jigme asked.

"Help you?" The old man peered up from under his brows.

"Yes, my mother's quite sick. I think I have to go and find someone who can make her well again. Can you tell me where I should go to?"

9

Great-uncle Rabten stared at the ground and tapped his walking stick on the dry mud. It was a long time before he spoke and Jigme was beginning to think he had forgotten the question altogether.

"If you follow the great river valley half a day's journey to the east you will come to a ferry. Take it across to the other side. There you will find a place where prayers are carved into some huge, white rocks. Follow the trail that runs around the hill behind them and you'll come to an old monastery set back out of sight. A very famous lama lives there. If you can get to see him I'm sure he could tell you what to do. I'm afraid my joints are too stiff these days or I'd come with you and show you the way."

The old man lapsed into silence and nodding to himself with his lips pursed was once more lost in thought. Jigme thanked him politely, although he was not sure his great-uncle heard him, and hurried back home. A feeling of great excitement stirred inside him. A journey! He would go on a journey across the great river and find a cure for his mother.

His dog was sitting on the doorstep of their house waiting for him.

"Little Leo!" Jigme squatted down and pushed back the fronds of hair that fell down over the small dog's eyes. "Tomorrow I'm going on a journey. I'd take you with me but you must stay behind and guard my mother. Will you do that?"

The dog wagged his tail and licked Jigme's hand.

It was time to make preparations. Jigme tried to think of all the things he might need: a few provisions – dried cheese, roasted barley, a bottle for drinking water, some silk offering scarves and a gift or two for the lama. He thought it might be a good idea to take his warm hat, and perhaps a slingshot too. He fingered the wooden catapult from the lowlands that he kept tucked in his belt. His eldest brother had given it to him. It was different from the kind they used in the high pastures but it would be very handy if he had to ward off aggressive dogs in strange villages.

He set about collecting the necessary things together. Little Leo stuck to his heels, following him everywhere as if reluctant to be parted from him until the very last minute. He watched with curiosity as Jigme helped himself in the kitchen, putting a few handfuls of grain, dried apricots and cheese into small, cloth bags and tying them tightly at the neck. He padded after him to the village store and back home up onto the roof where the boy laid everything out carefully in the sunshine, inspecting it all before packing it away in a striped shoulder-bag.

Finally satisfied he had done everything he could to prepare for an early morning departure, Jigme hung his bag beside the front door in readiness and went off into the fields for the afternoon with Leo to scare the crows and play beside the stream.

The next day by the first glimmer of morning light Jigme was already on his way on the road out of the village. He had left a note for his mother telling her not to worry and that he would be back soon. He had said goodbye to Little Leo and had left him in charge of the house. Then he had slipped out while it was still dark – before anyone could ask too many questions or try to stop him. He felt so pleased with himself that once past the last houses he sang and whistled as he walked, calling to the marmots in their holes, telling them it was time they woke up too. Gradually the sun rose high in the sky and a light breeze seemed to be chasing him on his way. From time to time he stopped to fill his bottle from a stream and eat some of his cheese, and by midday he had reached the great river.

It was a magnificent sight. Wide and smooth it swept its way eastwards, its course broken only in places by occasional sand bars far out in the middle. Willow trees clustered long its banks, stubbornly resisting the relentless tugging of the current washing over their roots.

Jigme picked up a twig and flung it as far as he could out into the water. In a moment or two it was gone, borne swiftly away downstream and lost in the bright reflecting sunlight. Jigme threw another and chased after it along the water's edge trying to keep level until it too vanished.

It was another hour or more before he finally reached the ferryman's cottage. There was no sign of the boat or the boatman, but the boatman's wife gave Jigme a bowl of butter tea and he sat down on a rock on the riverbank to wait. The sun was warm and Jigme was tired and after gazing out across the river for a while he fell asleep with his bag tucked under his head for a pillow.

The noise of dogs barking finally woke him. There was the boat, gliding towards the river's edge, the passengers getting ready to lift their bicycles and bundles ashore. Jigme perched on his rock and watched. Soon everyone had alighted and gone their separate ways. Only the ferryman was left talking to his wife. There did not seem to be anyone else besides Jigme who wanted to cross the river the other way.

Feeling a little awkward, Jigme waited. He did not think the boatman would want to go all the way back to the other side just for him. But his luck was in.

"Hey little brother!" the man called out to him, "If you want a ride, come and give me a hand."

Jigme hurried to join him.

"I've got to take this goat across and I can't manage it alone. There's a party of travelling monks on the other side too, waiting to come over."

The ferryman's wife appeared around the side of the house leading a brown and white speckled billy-goat on the end of a rope.

"He's a rambunctious beast. If you can keep a firm grip on him while I manage the boat I'll take you across for free."

The woman handed Jigme the lead and goat and boy looked at each other. The animal rolled its yellow eyes at him and curled its upper lip to reveal long, almost equally yellow teeth. It was quite a game persuading it to approach the boat. It dug in its hoofs, lowered its horns and grumbled every inch of the way as Jigme dragged it to the water's edge. Together he and the ferryman finally managed to lift it on board and they cast off.

It was wonderful out on the river. A light breeze played across the water and birds skimmed and dipped with it. Occasionally a fish would rise to the surface and disappear again with a splash, the sunlight glittering silver on the ripples left behind. But Jigme had far too much on his hands to bask in the beauty of the boat-ride.

The goat had got wind of something edible in the boy's shoulder bag and persisted in trying to nose his way into it. Jigme quickly sat on the bag to outwit it but discovered this was not the good idea he had imagined it would be. The goat put its head down and began butting him out of the way with such fierce insistence that they both nearly fell overboard. It was only after he had scooped a few surprise handfuls of water into the goat's face that it backed off a little and tried nibbling the edge of his coat instead.

Throughout the trip Jigme was either fending the animal off or trying to restrain it from climbing onto the side of the boat and tipping them all into the river. The ferryman was highly amused by the struggle going on at the other end as he sat in the stern skillfully steering their way through the strong current and finally into the shallows on the far side.

It was with great relief that Jigme handed the contrary beast over to its waiting owner, but as he set off up the trail away from the river it seemed as if the whole world still smelled of billy-goat. He wondered how long the odour would go on clinging to his clothes and flapped his arms wildly as he walked, hoping to get rid of it.

The carved white rocks were visible just as Uncle Rabten had said they would be. They towered above him on a prominent cliff that marked the opening to a small valley. The road divided at that point and a narrower track took off round the spur, winding its way up behind the cliff and out of sight.

Climbing the hillside Jigme took a last look at the great river snaking eastwards, before it was hidden from view. He thought he could just make out his own village far, far away on the other side. But the afternoon was hazy and he could not be completely sure. The ferryboat was already on its way back; a small oblong edging its way across the glistening water.

The afternoon passed and the valley below was already in shadow by the time Jigme came to the old monastery. Perched on the hillside with a sheer drop on two sides it was more like a fortress. An enormous black and russet mastiff lay sprawled at the front gate, eying Jigme with lazy consideration as he approached. The boy knew better than to go too close, so he halted a good distance from the animal and waited for someone to appear. He did not have long to wait. Heralded by wheezing and puffing noises an elderly nun appeared from behind the monastery wall carrying two buckets of water. She glanced sideways at Jigme without stopping.

"If you don't intend to rob or murder us, just step round him." The old woman gave a crackling laugh. "Mr. Lucky here can smell a good'un from bad."

She crossed the threshold into the monastery courtyard, gesturing with her shoulder for Jigme to follow. He approached the gateway cautiously and picked his way past the beast's huge, outstretched paws. The dog did not take its fierce eyes off him for a moment but in fact gave no more than a casual twitch of its nostrils as he passed.

Across the courtyard the monastery door stood open. Jigme paused on the steps to extract one of the silk offering scarves from his bag before going in. He folded it neatly and then stepped into the gloom. There was almost no light at all in the small hallway. He could just make out the outlines of larger than life size painted guardians peering down at him from the walls, and in front of him a giant pair of decorated gilt-iron door handles. Carefully he grasped them and pushed the doors open.

The pleasing spicy smell of incense spiralled around him and he found himself looking into the monastery shrine room. From the far end a golden statue of the Buddha gazed at him with a gently benevolent smile. Jigme bowed respectfully with his hands together and took a few steps forward. After the darkness of the vestibule the shrine seemed filled with light and at the far end against the right hand wall he could see someone seated on a low throne.

He made his way down an isle between rows of monk's cushions and feeling suddenly timid glanced hesitantly around to see if there was anyone else in the room. But there was only the golden Buddha with his undiminishing smile of kindness and the figure ahead of him dressed in the maroon robes of a monk.

When they were finally face-to-face Jigme had no doubt he was looking at the lama his great-uncle had spoken of. He was a very big man wearing an ornate pointed hat. His presence radiated power and ordinarily the boy would have felt quite daunted at having to speak to a person of such stature, but instead he felt himself enveloped by a comforting wave of warmth. The lama was quite old if not yet elderly and had a look of affectionate amusement in his eye as he observed his small visitor.

Jigme spread the white silk offering scarf over his outstretched palms and presented it as gracefully as he could manage, lowering his head as he did so. In return he received a sharp, little crack on the crown of his head from the lama's rosary. For a moment he was quite stunned and not only forgot completely what he was going to say but also almost what he was doing there at all. Then something moving caught his eye and brought him back to his senses. A small, sleek rat, as if hoping it was invisible, was picking its way slyly towards some scattered barley grains on the lama's table.

The lama laughed.

"It's probably not the only one who's hungry. You've come a long way today child and we can talk about your mother in the morning. Go to the kitchen and the cook will give you something hot to eat. He can give you a bed for the night too."

The lama gave Jigme a handful of sweets.

14

"I'm very pleased you came to visit. Get a good night's rest and come again at sunrise."

Jigme nodded and backed away slowly, his mind in a spin. He had not needed to say a word. It was extraordinary! By the time he was out in the courtyard once more he found himself propelled by an exuberance that totally overcame his fatigue. This was somebody special. He was sure he would know what to do. He let out a joyful whoop into the dying afternoon that made even Lucky the mastiff cock his head with interest, and sped round to the back of the building to find the kitchen.

There did not seem to be so many monks in the monastery but the soft, deep sound of chanting reverberating through the walls woke Jigme well before dawn. Later the cook gave him breakfast of roasted barley and tea and when there was enough light to see what he was doing Jigme sorted out the gifts he had brought for the lama.

He waited until the tips of the mountains were outlined with a pale golden halo before approaching the shrine room once more. The lama was sitting in just the same spot as the day before and the boy wondered if perhaps he had been there all night. Today however a grizzled, long-haired terrier nestled protectively on the cushion beside him and tilted its head inquiringly as Jigme made a ritual offering of the presents.

When it was done the lama told the boy to sit on a cushion in front of him and then leaned forward himself so his head would be more on Jigme's level.

"Last night I had a dream of a very old friend of mine," he said, "and it was no mere coincidence."

He paused and nodded to himself.

"This friend is not an everyday sort of person. In fact you'd have to search very long and very far to find anyone approaching him for skill in knowing the nature of things. He's a magician you see, and not an ordinary magician at that."

The lama's eyes were smiling and he began to run his prayer beads lightly through his fingers.

"A day's journey to the south-west in a valley hidden between two passes lies a poisonous lake. This friend of mine has taken up residence on a small island right in the middle of the lake. It's a strange place to live, but he's touchy about visitors. He likes to keep them at bay and it's an ideal place for doing that."

Jigme sat up straight, feeling the lama's golden, protective warmth all around him, and wondered what was coming next.

"It's quite clear to me," the lama continued softly, "that you have some special connection with this magician. I am a man of only limited understanding, but he could tell you exactly how to help your mother."

A bubble of protest rose to the surface of Jigme's mind. He was sure the lama was also a very wise man indeed, but then perhaps the magician knew more about medicine than he did. He waited to see what else the lama was going to say.

"You need to be strong-hearted and constant. If you're wayward, flighty, erratic, fickle, volatile, unreliable, shifty, shaky, heedless, capricious, indecisive or loose, it will get you nowhere. Or rather it will lead you into a lot of danger. But if you're firm you have nothing to worry about. What do you think? Are you steady?"

Jigme nodded hesitantly and then catching a certain look in the lama's eye tried to do it more convincingly.

"Good. If you set out now you should almost reach the lake by nightfall. Remember, if your intentions are pure, crossing the poisonous waters surrounding the island will not be a problem."

The lama turned and picked the dog up. Then he extracted a folded piece of paper from underneath his cushion.

"Go back to the river and follow it upstream until you reach a small willow grove. Then find a comfortable spot to take a rest and read this." He handed the paper to Jigme. "I've written you some instructions to help you find the way. Put it away safely so it won't get lost."

Jigme slipped it carefully into his bag. The lama smiled at him kindly and patted him on the shoulder.

"Well then, you'd better not waste any more time. If in doubt follow your nose!"

Jigme rose to his feet and thanked him, feeling a little reluctant at being dismissed.

"You are welcome to come and visit me again whenever you like." the lama added.

This thread of future invitation somehow gave Jigme courage and hoisting his bag on his shoulder he turned and made his way out.

The walk back to the river seemed to take no time at all, but it was a couple of hours before he came to the willow grove and by then Jigme was certainly ready for a rest. Most of the way had been across wide stretches of flat sand separated by dunes. It had been hard walking and he was glad at last to find some shade.

He threw himself down under the tree that seemed to have the biggest pool of shadow and was grateful for the slight breeze that came up off the river and ruffled the leaves overhead. He refreshed himself with some water from his flask and ate a piece of fried bread the monastery cook had given him. Then he took out the lama's note. With his back leaning against the tree trunk he unfolded the paper and spread it on his knees. It was covered with the most beautiful writing and carefully Jigme spelled out to himself what it said.

"Life is short. Do not forget
The risen sun must also set.
A lightning's flash, a falling star,
However young or old you are
Know life is brief; a rainbow dream.
Remember that the things that seem
So real can never
Stay unchanged, the same forever.
A tyrant's grip, a lovely face,
Both will vanish without trace.
When fortune smiles rejoice and sing,
But when she's leaving do not cling.
Trying to make things stay the same
Will only bring distress and shame.
For nothing lasts. You must be strong.
Do not lose heart when things go wrong.
Wish that your pain's enough for all
Poor suffering creatures, large and small.
This solid seeming world of form -
So rough and sharp, so chill and warm,

With ever-changing day and night -
Is but a skein of magic light.
Keep calm inside and you will find
The secret nature of your mind."

When he had finished reading it, Jigme sat staring at the paper a little blankly. He had imagined it would tell him which road to take – turn left here, right there – what landmarks to look for. But this said nothing like that. He read it again wondering if he had missed something and felt the presence of the lama all around him smiling at him. He was still perplexed.

He wound the paper round his fingers, rolled it into a tube, unrolled it and rolled it up again. He looked around, wondering what he was supposed to do next. The river stretched as far as the eye could see to the east and to the west. It was also very wide at this point, with no apparent way across. Jigme remembered the lama saying the magician lived in the south-west, and got to his feet to see how the land lay behind him. The willow grove consisted of no more than a few hundred trees and beyond them was a small valley that curved its way up into a steep bank of hills. It looked as if a stream, dotted with odd saplings along its banks, ran down the middle. It joined the great river not far from where he was standing. Beyond that the river was bordered by wide tracts of naked sand and dunes once more.

"Well I'm not walking across any more of that!" he said to himself, and turned his attention to the valley inland. It looked inviting and a little mysterious. He scanned the distant slopes to see if there was a village higher up but he could see no signs of any houses at all.

"He said "Follow your nose", so I shall," Jigme thought, and pointing himself towards the southern ridges he set off out of the willow grove and up the valley.

He made his way diagonally towards the stream at first, but discovered the ground on either side of it was in fact marsh disguised by thick, short clumps of grass. Knowing if he got his boots immersed by accident he would have the unpleasant experience of walking all day with wet feet, he skirted the central flatland and kept to the valley edge. There was no obvious trail. There were numerous, criss-crossing paths made by goats or sheep that had come down to take a drink, but it did not seem as if this was a route frequented by human feet.

19

Every so often Jigme raised the rolled up paper tube and squinted through it at the folding slopes up ahead, isolating a rock or a patch of shrubs to see if there was anything interesting there. Flocks of white clouds scudding across the blue sky overhead cast ever-changing forms of light and dark onto the hills like giant herds of horses racing across the landscape. It made Jigme wish he had his father's horse with him and he imagined himself galloping up the valley and reaching the end in no time.

Eventually the land narrowed and Jigme found himself climbing the sides of the steep gully down which the stream escaped from its source higher up. The various animal tracks converged into one path here. He followed it up and up, across small, fertile patches where the watercourse flattened and yellow and violet flowers grew, and upwards again. After a while he came to the spring itself, the water collecting icy-cold into a small pool before beginning its descent. Jigme halted to refill his water bottle and get his breath back.

Peering into the tiny pond he found in its blue-green, glass-clear depths swam a single little, spotted fish. It was probably no bigger than the boy's thumb, but the bright translucence of the water seemed to magnify everything below the surface and perhaps it was not even that big.

Jigme crouched down on his knees and elbows and watched it swimming round and round its silent world.

"How strange" thought Jigme, "I wonder how it got here all by itself."

"Are you lonely?" he asked out loud.

If the fish heard him it showed no sign and if the boy's head cast a shadow over the pool it did not seem to bother it. It swam on its ever circular journey with hypnotic and timeless grace. Whatever the effort of gently flicking its tail fin, it was recompensed by the sheer contentment of being there – or so it seemed to say.

Jigme straightened up.

"I'm alone too." he thought. "Am I lonely?"

Well he had not thought about it until now. He looked around at the hillside, the valley below him and the sky above. Apart from the fish there was no sign of any other living creature that he could see. He thought of his mother and wondered if she was missing him. A cloud drifted in front of the sun casting a chill over the landscape. He wished he had brought Little Leo along with him. Now he was conscious of himself, he did feel rather empty inside. He busied himself drying off his water bottle before putting it away in his bag. Just as he was brushing the dust and dry grass from his sleeves he was aware of a movement somewhere above him.

High on the upper slope something seemed to be making its way towards the top of the ridge. At first Jigme thought it might be a trick of the light and moving shadows, but when the cloud had passed and sunlight flooded the hill again he could see it was clearly an animal of some kind. It was too large for a woolly hare and the wrong colour for a fox. It was also too agile for a stray sheep.

He rolled the lama's paper up again and gazed down it, cutting out the surrounding glare and trying to pin-point the animal as it wove its way between shrubs and boulders. It was not easy. Whatever it was it was moving with nimble urgency and Jigme could hardly keep up with it in the small circle of vision the tube allowed. Then his chance came. The creature paused just for a moment on top of a rock before leaping across a small chasm and bounding to the top of the ridge. He could see now it was something large and feline. It could only be a snow leopard or a lynx.

In great excitement Jigme set out after it. The animal was only in sight for a few seconds more before disappearing beyond the skyline. He raced up the hill after it, scrambling between rocks and levering himself up on the steep bits by clinging onto tussocks of spiky shrubbery. It took him a little time but finally, panting and perspiring, he reached the top at the same spot where he had seen the animal cross over.

From here he could see that the climb he had just completed was nothing compared with what lay ahead. In front of him, separated from where he stood by only a relatively shallow dip in the landscape was a wall of mountains. They ran in a chain from east to west like knobbles on an old dog's spine. There was no way through them or round them for miles in either direction. The only way would be across the sunken meadow and then straight up.

For the first time it occurred to Jigme that he could have made the wrong decision right at the beginning when he left the willow grove. He had been so determined to avoid the sand-dunes. Now he was confronted by this vast inhospitable massif instead. He wiped the sweat from his face with the end of his sleeve and wondered which way the big cat had gone.

Then he saw it. It was sitting at the base of the escarpment sunning itself on a flat rock. He could see quite clearly now by its brown, freckled fur and its dark, tufted ear tips that it was a lynx. It was washing its paws, and every now and then there was a flash of white as it revealed the light, thick fur on its belly.

After a little it yawned, stretched itself and stood up. For a moment it remained motionless, inspecting the steep mountainside ahead. Then it turned and looked straight at Jigme. It was an extraordinary sensation. The boy felt electrified, terrorised, delighted and honoured all at once. He was pinned in the animal's fearless gaze. It swished its tail backwards and forwards a couple of times, made just the slightest movement in Jigme's direction and then fixed its attention on the mountain again. The boy watched it as it moved away uphill.

"I think it's telling me to follow it."

He began running down the slope and across the open, grassy field that separated him from the lynx's rock. There were no uphill trails that he could see. Ahead was a mass of shale and rocks with very little vegetation. Without any guidance he could encounter all kinds of dangers trying to cross such a high mountain. Although he was a little frightened he was sure the wild lynx knew the way up. This was its habitat. Jigme was anxious not to lose sight of it.

The lynx's coat was well disguised against the brown of the hillside, but Jigme could just make out its stealthy, silent form climbing steadily westwards up the mountainside. He tried to follow strictly to the course the cat was taking and set off after it examining the ground carefully for the occasional patch of fine dust that would reveal a paw-print and reassure him he was on the right track. He was heavier than the lynx and sometimes if he stepped on a loose rock it would slip and send an avalanche of small stones and dirt rattling down the incline below him. There was almost nowhere flat to put his feet and the strain of walking at an angle up the rough ground soon made his ankles ache. Occasionally he looked down and was encouraged to find he was gaining altitude quite quickly, but it as hard work.

The lynx was soon a long way ahead of him. Whether it needed to take a rest, or whether it was casually waiting because it felt Jigme was falling too far behind, he was not sure, but after a bit he could see it was sitting high up surveying the view. It stayed there for quite some time, giving him a chance to narrow the gap between them considerably and then take a rest himself.

So it went on. They crossed one ridge, descended into a narrow gully, climbed another ridge and just as Jigme was beginning to feel convinced he had been truly a fool to follow the lynx into this rocky wilderness, he noticed what looked like a path up ahead. It was not very wide, but as he got closer Jigme could see that it came from the West and ran like a ribbon, twisting and turning up towards the summit of the mountain above them.

Once his feet were on this small but well trodden track he felt an enormous sense of relief. Even if it did not lead directly to the magician's lake, this trail had to go somewhere. He stopped with his back against a giant rock and waited to get his breath back. From here he could see the day's progress laid out beneath him. The distant river looked quite insignificant, the willow grove no more than a grey-green blur.

"What a long way down," he remarked, looking at the tiny, glinting patch way below to his right. That had to be the fish's pool. The climb looked impressively steep from here. He was very pleased with himself. It was quite an achievement. He was just imagining himself telling a rapt audience of friends how he had climbed this harsh, strange mountain all by himself, when his reverie was rudely broken by something between a yowl and a hiss.

The lynx was sitting no more than a few yards away from him and looking at him rather crossly. He was instantly embarrassed. If it had not been for the lynx he would no doubt by now be completely lost, still slithering around on the dusty scree, trying to get a foothold.

"Thank you for helping me," he muttered rather awkwardly.

The big cat arched its back and stretched, looking somewhat mollified. Then with a single swish of its tail it turned and bounded away across the mountainside, vanishing onto the distant brown and speckled slopes beyond.

When he was fully rested, Jigme set off once more, happy this time to have a real path to walk along. It was a steep one however, and when an hour or so had passed he realised he was getting very weary. He trudged on. Again and again he thought when he reached the rocks up above him he would be able to see the next valley, only to find another, higher ridge to be crossed.

The afternoon passed and the sun sank slowly towards the horizon. At last, just as the sky was beginning to fill with the last orange glow of the day he struggled up the final ridge and found himself at the very top. He gazed down. Before him stretched a strange and beautiful vision of tumbling mountain streams and, far below, a lake, golden in the fading light. Although it was what he had been looking for, now that it was in front of him it was somehow so unexpected that he stood there spell-bound for quite some time.

He knew he couldn't reach it before nightfall, so he sped downhill as fast as he could until he found a rocky overhang. He brushed the ground under it clean with a bundle of twigs, crept in it as far as he could, and having eaten a little supper he slept a deep and contented sleep.

By daylight Jigme could see that the way down to the lake descended first through rocky scrubland divided by fast flowing streams, but that after that the slopes became steep and thickly wooded. The farther shore of the lake seemed to be covered with sand and grassland, but there was no easy way round to it that he could see. There was certainly a tiny island in the centre of the lake, so taking heart Jigme set off down the mountain side.

Before long he found himself struggling through increasingly impenetrable forest. The foliage overhead became thicker and the terrain underfoot more hazardous with each step. The more the sunlight was obscured, the harder Jigme found it to see where to put his feet. Any kind of trail had soon disappeared. In the dim dampness, picking his way down mossy boulders that wobbled under the slightest weight, his progress was slow and required great caution. His boots no longer had any grip on the slippery stones and tangled creepers appeared from nowhere as if purposely trying to trip him up.

The stillness of the morning had become full of strange bristlings and bustlings. Growls of displeasure somewhere below in the undergrowth were answered by hoots of derision from other creatures in the vines overhead. Something unseen crashed past him downhill, squealing and snorting as it went. In fright Jigme lost his footing and tumbled down the steep slippery incline, managing to catch hold of a small, rotting tree stump just in time to stop himself from hurtling onto some very jagged rocks far below.

Jigme lay still for a moment among the leaves, his heart thumping. Something in the forest with a furry kind of voice was laughing at him.

"Kit-kaat-kaat-kaat," cried a fork-tailed bird swooping overhead.

"Here you are-ja-ja," answered another.

"Why-tu-tu-why?"

"Chee-pur-weep. Chee-pur weep."

"Pu-pu-weer."

"Chip-prit-priichy-prit."

"Why-tu-tu-why?"

"Priichy-prit."

There were rustlings and scufflings among the dead leaves and then the soft, throaty laugh again, this time a little closer. Jigme scrambled to his feet in fear.

"Kit-kaat-kaat-kaat", insisted the bird, and everything grew silent.

He had no idea how much further down he had to go before he would reach the lake, but he was beginning to panic.

"Aaagh" went something in the bushes beside him.

"Nggaaargh!"

Jigme hurried on looking neither to right nor left. He could hear running water nearby and decided that following a stream would be the fastest way down. Soon he found an ice-cold rivulet cascading its way between the trees and slithered down the rocks beside it as best he could. Down, down he went. Something seemed to be padding along beside him, something large and unseen. Behind the bushes it was loping down through the undergrowth, keeping more or less level with him. At last, through an occasional gap in the trees he could see the glint of sunlight on water not far below.

"Back. Go-go-go-back!" chattered something scampering along the boughs overhead and a handful of hard little fruits rained down around his ears.

The stream disappeared underground. Once more Jigme was reduced to scrambling down from tree to tree and fighting his way through a wall of vines, thorn bushes and dead fungus-covered branches. The creature was close behind him now. The sound of it panting and chortling made the hairs on the back of his neck stand on end.

"Mine. Mine." it purred.

Again he glimpsed the lake below him, much closer now, shimmering in the sunlight.

"Back. Go-go-go-back."

"Mine. Mine."

"Kit-kaat-kaat-kaat."

Suddenly the undergrowth came to an end and before him was nothing but a mass of tree roots stretching down a steep drop and out into the lake. Some fifteen feet below him was a tiny patch of sandy beach.

"Mine. Mine."

"Nggaargh!"

Jigme jumped.

He hit the ground almost before he knew it. The sand was soft and embraced him when he fell, but nevertheless he landed with a terrible thump that took all the breath out of him. It was a few minutes before he was aware of the blue, blue sky overhead and the gentle lapping of the water nearby. Far off in the forest he heard a growl of disappointment followed by mocking laughter receding into the distance. Then the quiet of the warm day enveloped him.

He pulled himself to his feet and shook the sand out of his clothes. He was suddenly aware of how thirsty he was. The bright clear water rippled invitingly. Wriggling his arms out of his coat sleeves, he went to the edge of the lake. He cupped his hands and leaned forwards. At that moment two small pieces of dried cheese fell out of his pocket and plopped into the water. Instantly they began to fizzle and foam, an unpleasant purplish steam arising around them. Of course! The lake was poisonous. He had completely forgotten the warning he had been given. He leaped back, terrified at the danger he had been in. The cheese had been reduced in no time to a little patch of unpleasant looking scum that floated away from the shore and dispersed.

Jigme sank to his knees in disappointment. Behind him and on either side lay the invisible dangers of the jungle. In front of him the innocent looking lake offered certain death. A burning fury began to take hold of him and leaping to his feet again he started to roar and stamp like a thwarted forest beast himself. He howled at the beautiful sunny day that had turned so menacing, he kicked at the golden sand in rage and punched blindly at the invisible air.

"It's not fair! It's not fair!"

And finally exhausted he threw himself back on the ground in misery. He lay on his back with his eyes closed and watched the anger drain out of him. It was replaced by a great sadness. He saw his mother lying far away in bed, her eyes smiling at him kindly and little Leo sitting patiently beside her. And as he thought of his mother he was filled with a prickly shame. She needed his help, and here he was losing time and energy getting furious.

When he opened his eyes again the first thing he saw was a skinny, green frog sitting on one of the tree roots that stretched down across the sand into the water. Its bulbous eyes were fixed intently on him.

"So you're the one I'm supposed to be waiting for are you?" it said.

Jigme sat upright. "I need to speak to the old magician who lives on that island." He gazed out across the dazzling water. In fact the island wasn't so very far away at all and he could clearly make out the figure of someone sitting underneath a tree. "But I don't know how to reach him."

"That's what I thought." said the frog.

It somehow didn't surprise Jigme that the frog could talk. It had a soupy kind of voice that seemed to come from somewhere down in its stomach, just the kind of voice he might have imagined a frog would have, rich like gravy.

"I might just be able to help you."

"Oh, would you. Please."

The frog turned its slender back on him and started limbering up. It leaned forwards on its chin and kicked its back legs into the air in a series of pincer movements. It squatted on its haunches, puffed out its throat as far as it would go and flexed its shoulder muscles rhythmically. It performed an elegant succession of rapid jumps backwards and forwards sliced at the air in front of it with its splayed webbed feet as if combatting a mortal enemy and turned to face Jigme again.

"Alright, let's do it. Now the trick is not to wobble, and the best way to do that is to imagine you are following the smell of something delicious. Step exactly where I do"

The frog faced the lake.

"Stand behind me!"

The boy clambered up onto the gnarled tree root and looked out across the water, not knowing at all what to expect. The frog uttered an authoritative croak and sprang forward onto the surface of the lake. Precisely where it landed, the water parted neatly and revealed a hump of tree root below. Again it jumped and again the ripples divided to give it another piece of root to land on.

"Be quick. Don't dawdle."

Jigme looked apprehensively at the way before him. It was all very well, the surface area he was supposed to put his foot on might be big enough for a nimble frog, but what if his boot slipped? He had visions of his foot dissolving in purplish froth. What was it the frog had said? Conjure up a delicious smell and don't wobble. He thought of his mother's yak-meat and noodle stew simmering on the stove, stared at the lake and jumped.

Surprisingly there was quite enough room to land with both feet together on the root without getting even the smallest portion of his boots wet. He tried again. He remembered how the smell of roasting barley used to wake him when he was small and he used to lie curled up in his sheepskin with his eyes closed, savouring it. He jumped.

Then there was the wonderful rich aroma of dumplings frying. His stomach growled in hungry reminiscence. He hopped on. On a winter's day at school the smell of hot bread from the bakery next door was a constant distraction. His foot landed squarely on another protruding root. And occasionally when his father had been away on business he would bring back some special Chinese tea for his mother. It came in yellow packets and had dried jasmine flowers in it. The steam rising from her porcelain bowl had a delicate, pleasing perfume.

Jigme stepped onto the next piece of root and looked around him. The reality of where he was, quite far out from the shore now, and surrounded on all sides by poisonous water took him by surprise. He froze with fear. The frog was still ahead, plopping methodically towards the island, but he was suddenly incapable of moving after it. His legs seemed to have forgotten how to follow his instructions, and what was worse his knees were beginning to shake violently.

"Oh no! I mustn't wobble. I mustn't wobble."

The whole world seemed to be disappearing in dazzling whiteness and he had a terrible desire to just fall over sideways.

"I mustn't wobble". He cast about desperately trying to pull himself together. His mind was blank. He sniffed hard. He must think of a smell, something good, quickly. His brain seemed to be working with a terrible slowness. He sniffed again. Nothing. Nothing. Then somewhere at the very edges of the mid-morning air he thought he caught traces of something. It reminded of the New Year's holiday. He struggled to hold on to it. It seemed to be escaping him, but then with a surge of relief he found what had come into his mind and clung to it.

It was the smell of Juniper incense. He remembered the huge pile of sweet-smelling leaves and twigs burning in the monastery courtyard in his village. The fragrant smoke would curl up into the air to dispel any bad spirits that might create obstacles during the coming year. The monks would blow their trumpets. There would be crisp twists of pastry to eat and lumps of sugar crystal.

Jigme discovered his legs had stopped shaking and invigorated by the imaginary smell of mountain incense in his nostrils he stepped quickly and carefully forward onto the next spot where the frog had been, before the wicked waters could close over it.

It didn't take long to cover the rest of the way across the lake. A few yards from the island he stopped. The frog revealed the last place for him to put his feet, then dived into the lake and disappeared.

In front of him, underneath a fruit tree, sat an old man and a black and white dog. For a moment Jigme had the strange impression that the old man's body was covered in feathers. Then he decided it must have just been the effect of the dappled sunlight playing on his bare skin. The old man beckoned to him and with a hop and a jump he was on dry land.

"Did a young man help you across?" asked the old man, twitching his curly eyebrows suspiciously.

"Oh no," answered Jigme, "it was a talking frog."

The old man eyed him carefully and so did the dog, the breeze lifting the silky plumes on her ears.

"In that case you'd better sit down," and the old man made room for Jigme and pushed a few leaves together into a heap for him to sit on. "I expect you're hungry too."

Jigme had to agree that he was. The peculiar exercise of conjuring up different foods as he hopped across the lake had made him realise how empty his stomach was. The old man turned his back on him and started sifting through some dead leaves behind the tree. It was a very small island indeed. There was just the tree with a few fruit hanging on it and enough room for him, the old man and the dog to sit under it. Looking back across the calm lake at the jungly slopes beyond, Jigme marvelled at the all the terrors they had evoked. How still and peaceful it all looked and yet what dangers lurked below the surface.

"Here you are then."

Humming softly to himself the old man turned and handed Jigme a china bowl filled with juicy, steamed meat dumplings.

Jigme experienced a very odd sensation when he looked down. The bowl was exactly identical to the one his mother kept for guests on special occasions. It was white with a pattern of blue flames and dragons on it. Furthermore, the way the little pastry bags were fluted on top and the home made, spicy smell that wafted up from them was exactly as if they had been cooked by her too. His eyes prickled with tears and at the same time he tried to make sense of the fact that he couldn't see any sign of a fire, a cooking pot or any of the ingredients.

The old man started putting words to the jaunty tune he had been humming.

"Round and round the years go
Giant, ghost and man,
Goddess, demon, animal,
Do the best you can.

"A mother loves her children so,
Ugly, dull or mean,
She welcomes them with open arms,
No matter where they've been.

"A beetle sitting on the wall
Has had a mother too,
And if its mother's missing
Then it might as well be you.

"The vulture perching in the tree,
The snake, the bat, the shrew,
Have loved you once with all their might
So give them some dumpling stew."

Jigme put his bowl down. He picked a flat pebble out of the grass and placed it on top of a few golden leaves. Then he placed a dumpling onto the stone and took up his bowl again. There was an immediate whirring of wings, high pitched squawking, a scrambling and squabbling and the dumpling vanished.

"The world goes round, the stars go round, lifetimes go round," said the man. "This dear creature here has been the best and wisest companion anyone

31

could wish for. I can't tell you how many times she has prevented me from making selfish and foolish decisions."

He stroked the little dog beside him affectionately.

"But then we've known each other for thousands of years. Long ago I was her daughter in the arctic north. She used to carry me on her back in an embroidered sealskin pouch."

The little dog thumped the grass gently with her tail.

"Another time she was a powerful prince and I was the palace cockatoo."

He gave a crackling laugh and hunched his shoulders, and for a fleeting moment he was once more covered in pink and golden feathers. The little dog yawned and looked down as if she didn't approve of this kind of showing off.

"Alright, alright!" said the magician and patted her gently. "But most people think they'll live forever. They spend their time in an endless slumber – dreaming of moneybags and an adoring public."

He started singing again.

"The young men strut and swagger
When the actress passes by.
The mayoress bolts and bars her door
And dines off peacock pie.

"The army general's very grand
With medals on his chest.
The politician boasts a lot
And wears a cashmere vest.

"You've laced your shoes of crocodile
And put your diamonds on.
There's very little time left now,
You'll soon be dead and gone.

"So share your wealth with those who need
The things you hoard the most.
You never know what you'll be next -
A man, a beast, a ghost......"

By this time Jigme had finished eating his dumplings. The old man stretched out and took the empty bowl from him. He blew on it softly. The painted blue flames flickered slightly, the dragons wriggled a little and then the porcelain melted into a blue disc, as blue as the day, and vanished.

"And now for the really important matter – your mother. One thing I can tell you straight away. She's already feeling a little better. The very fact that you've been prepared to face all kinds of dangers for her sake has made a lot of other living creatures feel much better too."

He smiled.

"Listen!"

Jigme listened and became aware that the jungle across the lake was full of joyful, jubilant birdsong. It was so loud he was surprised he hadn't been aware of it before. Somehow he could tell that all the male and female birds were singing especially for their young. The air was thickly woven with threads of song so glorious, cascades of chirrups so encouraging, twitters of reassurance so sweet, that he knew even the most timid fledgling was inspired to stretch its tiny wings and try to fly.

"But enough of that for now."

The sounds receded into the distance again.

"The best thing you can do is visit an old friend of mine who lives a few days journey to the west. Most people think he's just a crazy drunkard."

He rolled his eyes and hiccoughed. The little dog wrinkled her nose in mock disgust.

"But he's not. Believe me. His mind is as clear as a mountain stream. Take him a jug of beer as a gift and tell him I sent you. He'll advise you what to do."

He slowly scratched the top of his head, then his armpit and casually produced from it a small, velvet, drawstring purse.

"Here, you should take this. It might come in handy."

Jigme thanked him and tucked it away in his bag.

"Cross to the far side of the lake and walk until you come to the main road. You'll find a tea-house where you can spend the night. Ask the owner how to get to the village where the salt traders go. That's where you'll find my friend."

He laughed and wagged his head at some private joke.

"Off you go now," he gave a toothy grin, "and don't come back!"

Jigme got to his feet and wondered nervously how he was going to get off the island again. Then he noticed a small boat moored behind the tree. A skinny green frog was sitting in the prow with its eyes closed, as if bored with waiting.

"Don't trail your fingers in the water. Keep your hands firmly in your lap," said the magician.

Jigme bowed to him and waved shyly at the little dog. She smiled saucily at him in return. Then he stepped into the boat and sat down. The frog opened its bulbous eyes, croaked fiercely at the water and the craft moved smoothly towards the shore.

The walk to the main road took a few hours, but Jigme's heart was light. He made up a song as he went.

"No one in the whole wide world cooks food like my mother.
I wouldn't swap her noodle soup – pom! pom! - for any other..."

And he had plenty to think about.

The journey to the salt village took Jigme three days. He travelled on timber lorries and tractor trailers and any other transport he could find. He met and talked to many strangers and answered many curious and nosy questions. But everyone was kind to him and helped him on his way.

The further west he went the flatter and dustier the countryside became. A vast plateau stretched out on every side. Trees grew fewer and very far between and from time to time he could see salt flats glittering in the sunlight. Eventually rocky ridges of hills began to rise up out of the landscape again and the bus Jigme was travelling on dropped him off within sight of the salt traders' village.

It nestled at the foot of a steep cliff and was surrounded by giant white and yellowish boulders ridged by wind and sand. Today, however, not a breath of air stirred. The sun blazed down with such ferocity it seemed to be defying anything on the face of the earth to move. It was only with the greatest difficulty that Jigme was able to put one foot in front of the other down the wide gritty track that led the mile or so to the village.

Sweat snaked slowly down his back and his boots felt like lead. As beads of perspiration broke out on his forehead a swarm of black flies appeared from nowhere and buzzed around his ears and eyes. He tried swinging his shoulder bag around his head to keep them away, but the effort of having to do both that and walk in the tremendous heat was too great. So he gave up and just plodded along the road, tossing his head from side to side like an irritated yak.

When at last he reached the village he slumped himself down in the first pool of shade he could find, with his back to a wall. All the streets were deserted. There was not even a dog to be seen, though he thought he could hear the faint sound of someone snoring inside one of the houses. He drank the last of his water and then fell into an exhausted slumber himself, waiting for the heat of the day to pass.

He was woken by the sound of a door opening in the house opposite him. An enormously fat woman began sweeping the dust off her doorstep. Jigme leaped to his feet and went to ask her if she knew how to find the magician's friend. She stared at him for a long time in a not at all amicable fashion. Then she gestured with her head towards the top of the cliff behind the village, spat into the street and slammed the door shut in his face. In the pale dust her spittle left a dark stain like a six-pointed star. Jigme thought of the magician and his dog and decided not to be disconcerted.

The day was as hot as ever. Nothing stirred in the dusty streets. He wondered if perhaps he should have bought the beer in the last town he had passed on the road. Then he remembered that the salt traders stopped off in this village and there would have to be a place providing refreshment for them somewhere. He wandered up and down the maze of lanes between the houses, and at last came across a large courtyard piled with sacks and bundles of straw. A doorway opened wide into a building at the far end. Jigme went in.

It was cool and dark inside. It was a moment or two before he could see anything after the glare of the yard, but as his eyes became accustomed to the lack of light he found he was in a large room full of men sleeping. Some were head down on the tables strewn with jugs and bowls. Some were stretched out on benches with their boots dangling. At one side in the gloom a young woman was sitting behind a counter rolling dice and yawning.

Jigme searched in his bag for the velvet purse. Among a number of smaller ones, there were three large coins in it. He took them out. The young woman looked up at him with interest.

"Hello! What are you after?" she asked.

Jigme put the three coins on the counter.

"I want as much beer as I can buy for these."

She looked at the money in amusement.

"That depends on what kind you want – best quality, second quality or the dregs."

"Oh, the best quality please."

She laughed.

"You're a bit young to be hitting the bottle, aren't you?"

"It isn't for me. It's for someone who lives up on the cliff top."

The young woman leaned her elbows on the counter and cupped her chin in her hands.

"Is it now?" she said, looking Jigme up and down with renewed curiosity. "Fancy that! That's pretty courageous of you. Lucky for you I threw a double one as you walked through the door or I might have tossed you straight out on your ear," She grinned and her earrings wobbled. "I can't cross a good omen like that."

Jigme looked down at the counter and the two dice with a single black dot showing on each stared back at him like a pair of eyes.

"Have you got something to put it in?" she asked.

Jigme shook his head.

"Never mind, I'll lend you a pot. One of the men can go up and collect it later."

She swept the coins into her apron and went off into the smoke-blackened kitchen.

The silence of the room was broken only by the buzzing of the flies and an occasional wheezing sigh from one of the sleeping men. Jigme found himself battling against a profound drowsiness. He shifted from one foot to the other and wondered if a sleeping spell had been put on the village. He rubbed his knuckles along the carved counter to keep himself awake and was glad when the young woman came back.

She dumped a large, wooden pot with a handle down in front of him.

"There you are. The very best. That should keep him happy."

She laughed. "Maybe it'll do us all some good. I hope so."

37

Jigme lifted the pot down carefully, thanked her, and stepped out into the blazing sunshine again.

It certainly had not got any cooler. He saw with relief that the pathway winding up the cliff behind the village was at least partially in shade. An hour or two had passed since the bus had dropped him off, and yet the sun seemed no lower in the sky at all. It was very odd and Jigme was glad to be leaving the village behind.

The narrow trail wound steeply up the cliff. It wasn't an easy climb. Sometimes Jigme had to squeeze himself around large forbidding boulders. He clung tightly to the handle of the pot, fearful of dropping it. There was no living vegetation, only occasional thorny shrubs, dried out and brittle. They caught at his clothes and he had to edge past them very carefully so as to neither get scratched nor lose his footing.

The way zigged and zagged upwards and from time to time he paused in the shadow of an overhanging rock to get his breath back. He avoided looking down. The heat made him dizzy and the sight of the long drop to the village made his head swim. Above him a large bird, black against the brightness of the sky circled lazily as if watching his progress.

Up and up he went and at last he reached the top. He found himself on a completely flat, dusty plateau and there, not fifteen yards away, was someone lounging comfortably against a tree. It was the only tree to be seen and looked completely dead, without a leaf on it. It stuck up in the heat like a crooked, withered hand.

"What a terrible spot," thought Jigme, and wondered why anyone would want to stay there. His boots stirred up little clouds of dust as he approached.

"There are places and there are places. But they're all the same to me," said the person before him cheerfully as if reading his mind.

He was a pleasant, bearded and rather ordinary looking man. He reminded Jigme of his uncle Nyima, the tent maker, except that he was sitting sprawled on a magnificent tiger skin.

Jigme put the beer pot carefully down in front of him and placed the palms of his hands together in respectful greeting. The magician's friend sat upright and clapped in appreciation.

"Terrific! You've brought some beer! What a hero! What are you? A giant disguised as a midget?"

He looked Jigme over.

"No you're just a boy. How amazing! Well, sit down, sit down."

He gestured at a folded sack and leaned forward to inspect the contents of the beer pot.

"Looks like a very good brew too. How did you pull that one off I wonder?"

He poured some out into an offering cup on a silver stand.

"She's a tricky one, that Tsering, and stubborn as a mule. She's just as likely to send up a bucket of ditchwater." He laughed. "Nah! She's not a bad girl really, but they're a bunch of fools in that village – always slipping rocks in the salt and short-changing each other. They think they're so clever. And when their beady eyes light on me they think they can criticise my drinking habits!"

He roared with amusement.

"Ah well, you've obviously got some powerful magic on your side too, or you couldn't have got so much as a drop out of her. But one good turn deserves another. What do you say? Let's let them off the hook, shall we?"

Jigme hadn't any idea what he was talking about and wriggled a little hesitantly on his salt sack to avoid having to answer. But he wasn't expected to answer anyway. The man turned his broad chest towards the sun. He raised his arm, uttered a few incomprehensible syllables and made a deft pass with his hand.

At once a light breeze enveloped them and the sun slipped a little towards the horizon. Jigme wasn't quite sure whether to believe his eyes. But there was no denying the feeling that the heat was off, or the relief that went with it.

"And now for a drink! I think you'd better pass on the beer and have a little of this instead."

He reached for a fancy, green flask with a glass stopper. "It's much stronger really, but it's legal for minors, midgets and magicians disguised as innocent boys."

He gave Jigme a teasing grin and handed him a tiny thimble-sized cup full of clear, colourless liquid. There was so little of it that before he knew it he had swallowed it in one go. It shot down through his body like a bolt of ice-cold lightning. It had the same effect as if he had just rolled naked in a snow drift. Every fibre of his body sprang awake. Every shred of fatigue vanished and the world looked intensely bright and interesting. His eyesight suddenly seemed so good he thought he could probably count the individual hairs in his companion's beard without even moving.

"Nine-hundred-and-eighty-four-thousand-six-hundred-and-twelve. " said the man. Then seeing Jigme was a little nonplussed he added "Hairs on my chin."

Jigme giggled.

As the sun lowered slowly in the sky and the man sipped at his beer they sat for a while in peaceable silence. Far below them the village, roused from its slumbers, echoed faintly with the sounds of goats bleating and men shouting. Above them the large black bird drifted idly in figures of eight.

"She told me you were coming," said the man watching its flight. "She's like my watch-dog. She can't help gossipping about everything she sees. Very useful."

Jigme wondered whether the bird was really a bird and whether it could talk like the skinny green frog. He remembered noticing the bird's black shape circling above him as he climbed the cliff, but it had made no noise that he had heard, human or otherwise. He watched it now, tilting its broad wings and resting on invisible currents of air. It seemed to be enjoying itself. Jigme's mind floated backwards and forwards with it. If what his companion said was true it was intent on the world below, its keen eyes observing anything that moved.

He glanced sideways at the figure next to him and the idea came to him that man and bird were completely at one. There was no question of gossiping. That had been a joke. Anything the bird could see the man could see too, sitting at ease beneath the leafless tree. The thought made him laugh and the man turned and smiled at him with such affection that it warmed Jigme's heart.

The sun set and the moon rose and the two of them dined together off dried yak meat and roasted barley flour with yoghurt. And as they ate Jigme told his new friend about his mother and his journey and the encounter with the magician on the island. And the man listened attentively, sometimes nodding in sympathy and sometimes snorting and chuckling into his beard.

The dusty landscape was transformed in the moonlight. It lay, pearly white and silver, as far as the eye could see. On the distant horizon the earth was separated from the sky by a rim of crystalline snow peaks, gleaming majestically in the night.

When Jigme had finished his story they sat again in silence for a long time. Finally the man reached for the empty beer pot, turned it upside down and began to tap on it with the tips of his fingers. The rhythm was intricate and mesmerizing and Jigme lay down on his back and gazed at the moon and the stars twinkling at each other. After a while the man began to sing, his deep, musical voice embracing the boy from head to foot.

"Things are not always as they seem at all.
Thick frosted clouds may hide the blue above,
Sweet words conceal a mind that plots your fall,
Ugliness clothe a heart that's full of love.

A handsome dog may please the farmer's wife
But flee in fear when wolves come near the farm.
And yet to save her owner's child from harm,
A timid seeming bitch may risk her life.

One who impresses with smart words at school
May falter when his feet must touch the ground.
Sometimes a man who seems an idle fool
Sees very clearly how the world goes round.

Keep your thoughts still, remember he who tames
His mind can see through all illusion's games."

The man's voice died away, coiling upwards into the night sky. And Jigme slept and dreamed he was a bird, swooping joyfully over the face of the moonlit earth.

He woke the next morning as the first shivers of dawn were appearing in the east. He was surprised to see in the half-light that the tiger skin next to him was stretching out its large clawed paws and bearing its teeth in a mighty yawn. As soon as it noticed the boy was watching it, it snapped its jaws shut and became nothing but a dried skin once more. Jigme rubbed his eyes with his knuckles. The man, who was sitting with his back to the tree and might not have slept at all, winked at him.

"Breakfast's ready." he said, pointing to a bowl of roasted barley flour topped with butter. He turned to pour out two cups of tea from a copper kettle boiling on a small fire next to him.

"You should make an early start before the day gets too hot. The person you need to see lives with this fellow's sister." He indicated the tiger skin under his feet and ran his big toe along its wonderful black stripes. "They live on the banks of a river in the south. I'm not sure exactly where. But in a village a few hours walk from here there's a yak that needs to be returned to its owner. Offer to take the yak home and you'll get the directions you need."

Jigme ate and drank his tea and wondered what the day had in store.

"Don't be afraid." said his companion. "We shall be looking after you, the bird, my tiger and I." and he gave him some dried meat and cheese for the journey.

Then he pointed out the direction the boy should take, gave his shoulder a friendly squeeze and as sunlight began to fill the sky, Jigme set out across the dusty plateau.

Some hours later the terrain dropped steeply down towards a river valley and further on the first signs of vegetation appeared. Lower still there were sheep grazing on the slopes and bubbling from the earth a spring that soon became a glistening stream. Jigme drank deeply and followed its course southwards with renewed energy. Eventually he came to a small hamlet, and there, tethered outside one of the houses, was a mournful looking yak.

He approached it cautiously, but it seemed quite docile. In fact it seemed to be a little pleased to see him and stretched its head forward for him to rub its nose. At that moment a young man came out of the house and looked at Jigme with surprise.

"I've come to take the yak back home." said Jigme confidently.

"Oh, is that it. We wondered when someone was going to come for it."

The young man bent down and felt the animal's leg under the thick mass of black hair.

"He's alright now. You'll have to take it carefully on the downhill stretches though. Make sure he doesn't slip. The muscle's still a bit weak. But I guess you can ride him sometimes if you want to. You're light enough not to make much difference. Come in and have some food."

Jigme followed him indoors. They sat down and a small girl served him a large bowl of noodles, which he devoured eagerly. Then while he washed that down with some hot butter tea, the young man took out some fodder, a saddle carpet, blanket and stirrups and got the yak ready.

"You know the way then?" he asked when it was time to go.

Jigme looked a little doubtful and didn't like to admit he hadn't the slightest idea.

"It's alright. If you get confused you don't have to think about it. This beast knows the way by instinct. He's been dying to go for days. Haven't you, old man?"

He stepped smartly out of the way as the yak tossed its large horns sideways in some kind of a reply.

"Good luck then. Go slowly."

And he watched as the boy led the yak off down the path.

The animal was clearly happy to be on the move. It was clear too that it didn't have to be led, so Jigme just held on to the braided rope attached to its nose-ring and strode along beside it. The hours passed and they headed away from the stream and up into vast tracts of grazing land, which swept the hillsides and stretched on and on into the distance. There was no visible trail, but the yak seemed sure of itself, picking its way diagonally across the immense slopes, and changing direction as if guided by signs that only it could see or hear.

Sometimes far up there were flocks of sheep making pale shifting patterns against the landscape, a dog or two running to chivvy the stragglers. Sometimes there were odd dark shapes of grazing yaks and Jigme's own yak would pause with momentary interest before plodding determinedly on.

Though the incline wasn't steep they were steadily gaining altitude. The air became fresher and thinner and as the evening approached there was a chill in the breeze. Still they kept moving on, the beast's thick skirt of hair glinting in the rays of the setting sun, the bell round its neck clinking with every step.

Jigme was tiring fast. It would be dark soon and he began looking out for somewhere they could stop for the night. Low down in a fold in the hillside ahead he spotted a large, natural depression that looked comfortable and sheltered. But the yak steadfastly refused to alter its course and investigate it. The grass was getting sparser the higher they went and the ground underfoot more loose and stony. They were approaching the summit of a huge undulating

44

ridge that arced westwards. A stiff wind was tugging and buffeting them. The yak, though its energy was flagging too, was flaring its nostrils and making soft appreciative grunts at the new smells in the air. Jigme guessed it must have detected something familiar and struggled to keep up until at last they were standing, panting and exhausted, on the top.

It was a flat area strewn with rocks. A small cairn of stones decorated with prayer-flags showed where other travellers had stopped and thanked the protectors for a safe arrival. Still out of breath, Jigme searched for a stone he liked, found a nubby, white one that reminded him of a conch shell and added it to the pile.

He accompanied the yak to the edge of the hilltop and sat down. They stared out at what lay beyond. They were much closer to the snow peaks now, pink and jagged in the fading light. In front of them the ridge dropped away into more pasture and grazing land, and to the right and left chains of dry mountains covered with shale stretched like arms enclosing it.

The yak was straining to be on the move again. It was time to get out of the wind and find a spot to sleep. Jigme got reluctantly to his feet. It was really very cold and night was almost on them. Jigme allowed the yak to pick their way down from the ridge. He remembered the advice the young man had given him about taking care of the yak's leg downhill, and kept a tight grip on the restraining lead. He was beginning to ache with tiredness and was worried that perhaps the yak was unstoppable and wanted to walk all night. It was almost dark now.

But he needn't have worried. Around a spur in the hillside they came across a perfectly sheltered place that had obviously been used countless times before for resting travellers. A dry-stone wall had been erected as a small enclosure for animals and there was a place for a fire, well-protected by boulders. The yak gave a satisfied sounding grunt, and trotted straight into the corral and settled down with its back to the wind break.

Inside his mind Jigme thanked the thoughtful herders who had left a neat stack of dried yak-dung patties against the wall for fuel. He set about making a campfire with them. There was no wood to add as they were well above the tree-line, so it was rather smoky, but it warmed him considerably. He gave the yak some fodder, then wrapped himself in the saddle blanket and sat with his back to a rock.

Beyond the small, glowing circle of the fire the night was very black. The wind was blowing relentlessly on the mountainside. It made strange keening noises as it whipped across the rocky slope. Jigme began to feel very much alone. The living world had vanished and he found himself straining his ears into the darkness. From time to time he thought there were other sounds within and beyond the wailing that rose and fell. For a moment he thought he caught the sharp whistling of a shepherd calling his dog and his hopes soared at the thought of company. But no one came.

Then there was the distant sound of falling water, like a steep, mountain stream cascading endlessly onto rocks far below. A man and a woman seemed to be having an argument nearby, on and on, backwards and forwards, though he couldn't make out the words. But coming out of the night was another much more persistent noise that he tried hard to avoid concentrating on. That was the sound of a baby crying. Perhaps it was a very small child abandoned and lost on the desolate ridge. Jigme felt agonised by it and hunched closer to the fire. He wished desperately he was back at home within the four, secure walls of his parent's house. He clapped his hands over his ears and tried to picture his father's smiling, friendly face. But the terrible, heartbreaking noise seemed to be just as much inside his head as outside.

"Amaa! A-ma! Amaa!"

Suddenly a freak gust of wind swept straight down into the fire and sent the thick smoke swirling and choking into Jigme's face. He buried his head into the blanket, the fumes burning his throat and making his eyes stream. He waited a minute or two before cautiously surfacing again and there to his horror, peering over the boulder opposite was the most hideous and repellant creature he had ever see. His body prickled all over in terror.

Its hair was streaming out in all directions and its eyes bulged. Its mouth was wide open to reveal fearful, sharp fangs and it stared straight at Jigme and licked its lips. The crying sound seemed to be issuing from its throat, but it wasn't a child at all. Rather it was something old and very, very wicked. Jigme knew he should flee for his life, but his whole being was paralysed. Not a sound would come from his throat and the pit of his stomach was stricken with an icy coldness. The demon, for that was surely what it was, was waving handfuls of bloody entrails and an awful, rotten smell pervaded the air.

Jigme sat transfixed, incapable of defending himself. The creature was

eying him with hungry anticipation, a triumphant smirk of amusement on its ugly face. It scrambled its way up onto the rock, blood dripping from its fingers, its nostrils flaring. For a fleeting moment Jigme thought miserably of the poor yak and wondered if it was already dead. To his left something striped snaked across the ground at the edge of his vision and instinctively he jerked his feet in, his heart pounding. It occurred to him there might be more of these maleficent creatures. Perhaps he was surrounded. What if there was a whole pack of them? He clenched his fingers to try and stop himself shaking, his nails digging into the palms of his hands.

"Mine! Mine!"

The sound roared out into the night. It was so unexpected that Jigme's heart almost stopped altogether in alarm. His mind and his vision blurred with confusion. Then something strange happened, as if he had been grasped roughly by the shoulders and given a good shaking. With a tremendous flood of relief he recognised the noise for what it was. The cliff-top tiger was there to protect him. All his courage returned in a great wave of heat. He took an enormous breath and sprang to his feet.

"Go away!" he shouted. "Go away, you evil cowardly thing! Leave us alone!"

"Ngaargh!"

"You can't stop me! I've got something important to do!"

Jigme hurled the words at it like weapons.

"Go away! I never did anything to hurt you!"

The creature leered at him and drooled. It was emitting a truly horrible smell – rank and putrid.

"Besides you really stink," he added, and then, inspired by something he had once heard his auntie say to his cousin, "You should try taking a bath. No girl's going to fancy you if you smell like porcupine's piss."

The effect was instantaneous. The demon faltered, a look of dismay spreading across its features. The glow went out of its eyes and was replaced by a shifty, shrinking look. Its breathing became laboured and its shoulders, which a moment before had been bristling with aggression, began to grow thin and powerless as it tried to cower back behind the rock again.

"Yugh!" Jigme grimaced and held his nose.

The demon began to look quite pathetic, but Jigme felt it was the wrong moment to show pity and continued to frown at it as fiercely as he knew how.

48

The nasty thing hesitated a moment longer and tried waving a piece of dripping intestines at him for effect. Then it gave up, sniffed disconsolately and vanished, leaving behind nothing but a faint, disgusting odour.

Jigme shivered with relief. Where previously there had been an agonised shrieking resounding in the night, the empty darkness was now filled with a deep rumbling purr instead. He was incapable of uttering another sound himself. The remains of his fear somehow made his tongue stick to the roof of his mouth, despite the fact that the demon was gone. But he stood for a moment looking out across the embers of the fire and thanked the man and his tiger with all his heart. Then, taking up his blanket, he stumbled into the corral and fell into an exhausted sleep, with his arms twined in the yak's thick, warm hair.

He woke late the next morning. The yak, impatient and hungry, finally managed to rouse him by snorting breathily down the back of his neck. It was a glorious day. As he straightened out the saddle blanket and fixed the stirrups in place he found it hard to believe how dreadful the night before had been. The air smelled fresh and exhilarating and a pile of beautiful white clouds were pillowed up on the horizon.

He considered the possibility that he might have dreamed it all. There was no sign around the fireplace that anything unusual had happened, but the impression left on his mind by the demon's evil face was so strong that he felt in the end that it didn't really matter much whether he'd experienced it awake or asleep.

He led the yak round the stone wall and stopped. There in the dust outside was the unmistakable imprint of a huge tiger's paw. Or at least he thought he saw one. It was there just for a moment before the yak's hoof stepped on it, scattering the earth and obliterating it completely.

They picked their way carefully down the first steep part of the hillside and were once more in long, green, undulating slopes. Further on there were meadows dotted with alpine flowers and the grass was so bright and lush Jigme thought it looked good enough to eat. Then he smiled to himself when he realised this was probably what sheep and yaks thought every day of their lives. There were quite a lot of animals to be seen now grazing peacefully. The yak

was showing obvious signs of excitement and he knew they must be nearing its homeland.

It wasn't long before a small group of nomad tents came into view, and once they were within twenty yards or so of them the yak gave a vigorous shake of its head, wrenched the braided rope out of the boy's hands and wandered off to browse happily nearby.

Jigme walked up to the nearest tent and looked in. He was greeted by a burst of furious yapping. He flattened himself against the canvas flap as a red mother dog told him in no uncertain terms to stay away from her puppies. An elderly woman was busy making butter in a big wooden churn, and it was some minutes before she paused and looked up at him.

"I've brought a yak back." said Jigme. "Is it yours?"

"It is indeed." said the woman.

She wiped her hands on her apron and came to join Jigme at the opening.

"That was very kind. Would it be too much to ask you to unsaddle him for me?"

Jigme did as he was asked. He put the blankets and the tackle inside the tent and sat down to rest on a leather trunk and watched the woman continue her work. Later her daughters came in and he was given some tea and food. Women from the other tents came and went, but apart from greeting him in a friendly fashion none of them stopped to talk to him. They were all too busy with their chores in and around the camp site. It was only after they had milked the sheep and the goats and the men had come back for their evening meal that Jigme thought he might get a chance to ask a question or two.

He sat at a small wooden table next to the other men, full from his second meal of the day. The family of herders chattered together and he felt warm and comfortable. After his terrifying night on the mountain, the homely atmosphere was just what he needed. When there was a lull in the conversation he finally found an opportunity to speak.

"Please, does anyone know how to find the man with a tiger?"

This provoked a good deal of laughter and joking. Although one old man claimed he'd once been kicked by a tiger's hoof, none of them had ever seen a living tiger.

"There must be a story to this." said one of the daughters. She'd been observing Jigme in the firelight and wondering where he had come from.

51

"Tell us why you're looking and maybe we can help."

So Jigme told them of his journey. Everyone listened with interest and when he described his ordeal of the night before they looked at him with amazement and not a little respect.

"You mean you actually saw the demon of the crag?"

"And you lived to tell the tale! Aie! Aie!"

"There's more than a few who haven't."

"Old Phuntsok lost twelve sheep up there last autumn."

"It even picks grown yaks off the mountain and tosses them over the edge like empty barley bags."

"D'you remember that fellow from Lhasa, spent the night up there alone – never the same again. Went crazy."

"How big was it?"

"What did it look like?"

They peppered him with questions. Only the old lady didn't say a word. She sat by the stove, her rosary clicking softly through her fingers, her eyes on Jigme like some watchful bird. Eventually she spoke and everyone fell silent.

"Last winter, just after the new year, the weather turned very bad. One afternoon it started snowing quite heavily. All of you were out looking after the animals and making sure they were alright. While you were gone a wandering monk came to the tent and asked to take shelter. I was busy cooking and he came and sat near the fire to get warm. He said he was on a pilgrimage to the temple of Samye and when I asked him how long he'd been a monk, he told me a strange story."

"It seems he hadn't been a monk for very long. For many years he'd been a trader and his speciality had been animal skins and furs. He said there was a good market for antelope and he could make even more money on tiger and snow leopard skins. He used to travel the length and breadth of the country buying them from hunters and taking them to the big city to sell. At a certain time of the year his travels took him to the sacred, green valley in the south. This particular season he had very little luck there. The forests had become much smaller than they used to be, and the wild animals fewer and fewer."

"It looked as if he would have to return empty handed, but one day, when he was resting on the banks of the river, he was approached by a very poor and simple-looking couple – a man and a young girl. Their clothes were patched and ragged, and he thought at first they were beggars. But then they pulled out of their bag an enormous female tiger skin. It was one of the best he had ever seen. It was soft and supple, with glorious stripes and a long impressive tail. He had great difficulty containing his excitement, but because the couple were obviously so poor, he thought he might get it very cheaply. He offered them far, far less than it was worth, and after a little bargaining they settled the deal and he bought it."

"Later that evening when the trader was camped in the forest he decided to take the skin out and have another look at it. He unrolled it beside the fire and, to his horror, as soon as it was spread out on the ground it came alive and sprang on him, pinning him to the earth with its giant paws. As it breathed in his face with fury, he was sure his life was at an end. But at that moment the man and the girl who had sold it to him appeared and called the tigress off. They no longer looked ill-kempt and pathetic. In fact they shone with a kind of dignity and wisdom, and he felt very ashamed of himself and stupid."

"He sat up nervously and saw that the little forest clearing was full of animals – ibex, antelope, lynx, snow leopard, marmot – all jostling to get a good view of him. Their intelligent eyes and their silky fur gleamed in the firelight. He looked at them with great sadness, and knew without being told that every one of them was a skin he had bought and sold at some time. They seemed to bear him no ill will. Their look was concerned rather than reproachful, and it made him feel small and mean and very disgusted with himself."

"After a little, the animals disappeared among the trees, and the man and the girl sat down on either side of him. They sat in silence. He was too miserable to speak himself and too mortified. But he began to feel their presence was sympathetic rather than condemning. It was as if they were trying to show him something. He saw the world and how exquisitely beautiful it was, so full of light and magic. He saw himself as a boy surrounded by his parents love. Then he saw how little by little he had devoted his life to using the things around him, not in a way that benefitted the world, but simply for his own ends. Greed and need had made him take what was precious and use it to satisfy his never-ending desires, destroying it in the process. He had traded in death. He had given nothing in return. He hadn't even used the money to benefit anyone other than himself. What a lot of dead animals. What terrible waste. His eyes filled with tears and he sat reflecting on the past with great misery."

"He didn't notice when the man and the girl left. He only found at some point that they were gone, and laid at his feet was a scarlet flower that the girl had taken from her hair. He left the next day and travelled back north to his home village. He gave away everything that he owned and took the vows of a monk. After that he set out on foot to spend the coming years visiting holy places all across the land. He wanted to try and make amends for his willful ignorance."

"And that was the end of his story. I gave him some food and said he was welcome to stay with us for the night. But as soon as the snow stopped he thanked me and left."

The old woman paused. There was complete silence except for the sound of the wind outside and the intermittent crackling of the fire. Then she looked at Jigme again.

"I'm quite sure the man he met with the tiger skin is the one you're looking for. You must take the road down to the green valley in the south and search the banks of the river. I'm sure you'll find him."

At that moment there was a loud bang from the cooking fire and a tiny piece of red-hot wood flew out and landed right at Jigme's feet. Everybody laughed.

"There, you see, the fire agrees! That's a lucky sign for sure!" said the oldest herder.

The next morning Jigme got to ride on horseback with some members of the nomad camp. They were leaving the grazing land for a market town a day away. From there he was offered a lift in a truck with some of their cousins who were taking wool down to the low country. He accepted gladly.

Padded by the soft sacks and bales he bounced his way along the rough, dirt road that crossed the upland plateau. Later, as the miles went by, the landscape began to change. They left the vast empty spaces and began a long, long descent through a wide, steep gorge. The blue sky vanished as they plunged into thick, white mists. Tall trees dripping with moss loomed into view and vanished again. Small streams spilled out of the rocks, ran across the road and disappeared down into the unseen depths below. It was chill and eerie. Jigme had never in his life seen anywhere so damp. The whole world seemed to be full of running water like a thousand whispering voices. The road twisted and turned, jolted and bucked, on and on. It was impossible to see for more than a few yards in all directions. Hours passed and still they travelled down and down in the gloom.

At last gaps in the mist appeared and it grew perceptibly warmer. By nightfall they were well out of the damp clouds which now hovered above, hiding the way they had come. The next day the valley widened and soon they were passing through small villages and the hillsides were dotted with farmhouses. It was humid in this country and full of unlikely smells – rotting apples, sweet treacle, black tobacco, toasting bricks.

Lolling among the wool sacks, Jigme slept through the afternoon and woke again to find they were entering a large town. The streets were lined with beautiful trees covered in blue flowers. The houses had red, tiled roofs and the roads were busy with bicycles and motor cars, bells, horns, cows and confusion. The truck parked at the back of a busy bazaar just after nightfall.

Jigme waited until the following day before venturing out on his own.

"We'll be going back again after three days if you want a lift," the driver told him. "If you get lost ask for the Bhote Bazaar. You'll find us here until then."

The boy had no idea where to go, but it was early morning and he set off through the town in good spirits. Temple bells were ringing. The women were out filling their brass pots from dragon shaped waterspouts. Village people were setting up their baskets of fruit and vegetables on the roadside. There was no traffic yet and everyone seemed happy and at peace with the day.

Following his nose he came eventually to a large square and, choosing a temple with carved wooden pillars, he sat down on the steps and watched the world going about its business. He had hardly been there for ten minutes when a pretty girl made her way across the square towards him. She looked as if she was no more than twelve or thirteen years old and had a crimson flower tucked behind her ear and a long violet coloured skirt. She came and stood before him at the bottom of the steps.

"Hello. Baba told me to come and find you," she said. "You were pretty easy to spot. You look quite different from everyone else. No one I know has boots like that."

Jigme looked down at his dusty felt footwear and laughed.

"Come on. He's waiting for you."

She led him off through narrow, winding streets, into several inter-connecting courtyards, then down a long, unpaved alleyway. It ended at an open area on the edge of the town overlooking the river.

"I'm going to have to blindfold you now. No one's allowed to know the exact way." she said and began unwinding a strip of cloth from around her waist.

Jigme was suddenly very nervous. He wasn't sure he liked this. He looked around him. There was no one to be seen close by, only some farmers out irrigating the vegetable fields on the far side of the river. He wondered where the girl intended to take him, and whether it was a trick. He looked at the early morning sky of pale turquoise and was suddenly reassured. High above a black bird was making lazy patterns to and fro. Of course there was no saying it wasn't just any bird out of thousands, or even millions, but Jigme let the girl cover his eyes with the cloth and tie it tightly behind his head. It smelt of some peculiar musky perfume.

"Now turn around three times."

The boy did as he was told.

"Take hold of this."

She put something in his hand. Jigme couldn't tell exactly what it was. It might have been a silk braid. Or it might even have been a plait of hair. He held it firmly.

"Now I'll lead you. Follow me."

She gave a little tug and he set off cautiously after her. The ground underfoot felt very smooth at first. Then it became soft like fine grass. He grew more confident. There didn't seem to be any stones to trip over or stub his toes on. The sweet, exotic scent in his nostrils began to make him feel quite light-headed. He thought for a moment there might be no earth under his feet at all.

They didn't walk for very long and when they stopped Jigme could sense that the river was quite close by. The girl carefully untied the cloth, wound it around her waist again and ran off as fast as she could, disappearing among some bushes.

He stood there in surprise, rubbing his nose and looking around him. He was in an entirely different place altogether. There were no vegetable fields, no houses and certainly no signs of the town in any direction.

He wondered what he had let himself in for. But it was too late to turn back now. Carefully he walked between the bushes following the way he thought the girl had gone. Almost at once he found himself on the riverbank and there in front of him was a man leaping up and down on a tiger skin. The girl was peeping out at him from behind a guava tree.

Jigme wasn't sure whether the man was dancing or performing some complicated kind of exercise. Whatever it was, it was very impressive. His body seemed to be made quite differently from Jigme's body. Old as he was, he could bend it this way and that like a young willow in the wind. Sometimes his feet seemed to come up over his shoulder in a most surprising way.

Jigme stood watching with his hands clasped behind his back as the Baba pranced and twirled. All kinds of animals came into his mind: a dog chasing its own tail, a baby calf gambolling in the pastures, a water bird trying to impress its mate, a cat stalking its prey. It was fascinating. There was something wonderful about the grace with which the man moved. It looked completely effortless.

"Come on! Come on!" the Baba called over his shoulder in mid-arabesque. "Now you do it too!"

"Oh! I don't think I could do that." said Jigme a little awkwardly.

"Why ever not? It's only a question of letting go of all your fixed ideas."

"Can't do this,
　Can't do that,
　　Too old
　　　Too young
　　　　Too thin
　　　　　Too fat.
　　　　　　Relax your mind,
　　　　　　　Your hopes and fears
　　　　　　　Raucous laughter,
　　　　　　　　Silent tears.
　　　　　　　　Stand on tiptoe,
　　　　　　　　　Give a shout and
　　　　　　　Turn the whole world inside out."

58

The Baba threw his arms up above his head and stopped. For a long, long moment he seemed to be frozen, caught in time, poised somewhere between the earth and the sky. One toe was not quite touching the tiger skin laid out on the grass, the other foot was up behind his ear. He wasn't quite flying either and it seemed as if the whole world had stopped with him. Not a breath of wind shook the leaves. The birds paused in mid-song and the shimmering, babbling river was still like glass; each gleam a bright and frozen rainbow.

Awestruck, Jigme watched. Slowly he felt a surge of energy begin to ripple through his body. It gained speed. His fingers and toes began to tingle. His rib-cage trembled. His lips quivered and all by itself a great shout of spontaneous laughter bounced up out of his chest into the sunny morning.

He laughed. The Baba laughed. The girl behind the tree laughed. And out of sheer joy he danced a dance not unlike the Baba's. But it was a dance all his own, with his felt boots kicking up behind and his coat flying. He pirouetted up the bank one way and hopped back the other. He tripped over tussocks of grass, bounded over boulders and just missed falling in the river. He spun, cavorted, shimmied and finally collapsed in a heap at the foot of the tree completely out of breath.

The Baba, who had been sitting on a rock watching this performance, applauded.

"There you are you see!"

Jigme knew it was not quite the same as what the Baba had been doing, but he was pleased anyway.

"I'll say one thing for you; you're a tryer. You don't give up at the first kink in the road."

Jigme lay on his back panting with his eyes closed and listened to the gurgling of the river and the chattering of the birds among the guavas. The Baba sat on his rock and scrutinised him thoughtfully.

"Well! Well!" he said eventually, "We'll have to see how to help you. What do you think, Lily?"

The girl stood up.

"I think he's a very funny boy and I think he should stay here with us for ever."

"Well that's an idea. It won't do his mother much good though, will it?"

Jigme opened his eyes. The way they were looking down at him made him feel like something unusual that had been washed up on the river bank. But he had no doubt at all that they would help him.

Lily knitted her eyebrows and put her head on one side.

"No, that's true."

She held out her hand and helped Jigme to his feet."

"Then let's make a sand circle and see what answer that gives."

They went to the edge of the water and walked a few yards upstream where there was a small patch of silvery sand, bordered by reeds. They cleared away a few loose stones and pebbles. Lily took a stick and drew a big circle on the ground and they sat down around it.

Then Lily and the Baba began to construct a complicated diagram inside the ring. With pointed reed stems they carefully drew gateways and chambers, protecting walls and magical letters. It took a long time and looked quite remarkable when it was finished, like the blue-print for a magnificent palace.

"Now you have to take a bath," Lily told Jigme.

So he went down river a little way, took off his clothes and jumped in the water. After running around on the bank until he was dry he dressed and returned to the circle.

"Take this."

Lily took the scarlet flower from behind her ear and put it in Jigme's hands.

"Now you have to stand here. I'm going to cover your eyes and you must throw the flower into the circle."

She stood behind him and he felt her cool fingers gently closed his eyelids. He held the bloom by its stem for a moment, pictured his mother sitting on her red quilt, and tossed the flower into the air. It made a soft plop as it landed on the sand. Lily took her hands away.

It had fallen well within the outer rim of the circle, a little to the West where a strange squiggle had been drawn. The Baba leaned forward on his knees and examined it. Lily squatted next to him and together they discussed its position and what it meant.

"The stalk is pointing exactly towards the centre, look."

"And it's face upwards too. Very fortunate."

"It's completely covering the naga-serpent's tail, though, and part of the lotus paradise."

"Yes his journey isn't over yet."

The Baba knelt musing over it a little longer, nodding to himself, then somehow satisfied he got to his feet. Together they stood at the margin of the river and, bending down, scooped up handfuls of water and threw them over the sand. The lines of the diagram soon all ran together and vanished, leaving behind nothing but a glittering patch slightly darker than the rest of the little beach. As they turned to leave a sudden eddy from the river swept out across the place where the circle had been, hooked the crimson flower off the bare sand and bore it off down stream. For some reason this pleased Lily very much and she clapped her hands in delight.

They went back to the guava tree and in its shade she prepared them each a plate made of leaves with different kinds of food on it. It looked very strange to Jigme. There was almost nothing he recognised. There were peculiar orange tangles of fried batter soaked in syrup. There were vegetable fritters, but what kind of vegetables he could not tell. Their taste was unknown to him. There was a little pile of roasted grain mixed with such strange spices that his ears itched, and there were a few sleek, black fruits with purplish-scarlet flesh inside. He did not know what order to eat anything in, so he ate a bit of this and a bit of that and in the end felt quite queer.

"You should see the look on your face!" said Lily, laughing so hard she got the hiccoughs.

Jigme was offended. What did she know about anything, he thought crossly and pushed the food around with his forefinger. He didn't want to be part of her silly games any more. He felt terribly tired and suddenly his eyes filled with tears as a great wave of homesickness swept over him. It seemed months since he had left the village and he longed for familiar faces and familiar smells.

He pretended to look for crumbs that had dropped down his shirt front. He did not want her to see he was crying, nor the Baba either. But it was impossible to hide anything from the two of them. They were beside him in a moment trying to comfort him.

"I'm sorry" said Lily, "I didn't mean to laugh at you. I forgot how sad you must feel inside. I cried for hours last week when a monkey stole my earrings and bit me when I tried to get them back. Look." She pulled back her sleeve and pointed to a little line of blue-black teeth marks on her arm.

"Yes, well you shouldn't have been teasing it in the first place." said the Baba. "Enough of your nonsense, girl."

He stood up and stretched himself and looked at Jigme.

"Your mother's lucky to have a son like you and you mustn't go losing your grip yet. One thing you should know: the world is full of people garbling easy solutions to the problems of others. Three months flicking through a few books and they set up practice as a doctor. Two weeks sitting on a feather cushion and they're an enlightened, spiritual teacher. All bogus! You have to know how to deal with your own problems before you can sort out anyone else's. Don't trust too easily, and if in doubt look for signs and omens."

The Baba scratched his eyebrows, first one and then the other, and looked quizzically at Jigme.

"I don't know why I'm telling you this. You probably know more about it than I do.!"

He smiled and began to twirl slowly on one foot.

"The best thing you can do to help your mother is to go and visit a friend of mine. He and his wife are arrow makers. His mind is so sharp it will pierce to the heart of the problem straight away and his wife is a woman of great wisdom. You won't have any difficulty finding them. They're famous. Kings, warlords and hunters come from hundreds of miles away to see them. But they won't always sell their special arrows, no matter how much they're offered. You can be sure you'll find them tomorrow if you look. Lily will take you back to the city now. Go safely and good luck."

He was whirling around quite fast now, and as Lily began to cover Jigme's eyes with the cloth again, he could hear the Baba chanting:

"Turn the whole world outside in.
　　Find the end
　　　And then begin.
　　　　Float up river,
　　　　　Grasp the flame,
　　　　　　Change direction,
　　　　　　　Take your aim.
　　　　　　　　In joy or sorrow,
　　　　　　　　　Rage or bliss,
　　　　　　　　　　Can do that
　　　　　　　　　　　And can do this......"

Once more Jigme felt Lily place the silky braid in his hand and they set off away from the river. He was determined this time to try and pay attention to what exactly was happening. He could hear the grass scrunching softly under foot for a little way, but was suddenly distracted by a subtle and momentary lurch as if he had fallen very fast from a considerable height, only to be met by firm, soft grass beneath his boots again. Lily was humming softly as she led him along and a light breeze was playing with the tails of his blindfold. He had no sense any more of whether they were going up or down or even round in circles, and it was really quite pleasurable. It occurred to him that he was probably better off not trying to concoct explanations for the inexplicable.

Eventually they came to a halt and Lily set him free and untied the cloth. They were on the outskirts of the town once more and the fields below them looked pink and yellow in the late afternoon light. Lily pointed across the valley to a low hill on the far side.

"The arrow maker lives on top of that rise," she said. "You should go there first thing in the morning. Later in the day he might not be there. He goes into the forest to look for feathers."

She took Jigme by the shoulders and turned him around.

"There's the gully that leads back into the centre of town. Walk straight ahead and don't look back. Oh, and if you come to visit us again, next time bring me some corals and turquoises and I might marry you!"

She kissed him lightly on the cheek and gave him a shove to set him on his way.

Jigme hurried off towards the houses as he felt his face begin to burn. There was certainly no chance he would look back now, far from it. For a long time afterwards he could feel a sensation where her lips had touched him, light and fleeting like the brush of a rabbit's ear.

Jigme spent the night in Bhote Bazaar with the truck driver and his friends and set off out of the city again at dawn. He crossed the river on a rickety bridge made of planks balanced on large stones. It wobbled alarmingly as he walked and he was happy to reach the other side without falling in. The pathway beyond ran along mud ridges between vegetable fields and before long he was climbing up the lightly wooded slopes on the edge of the valley. The way meandered round and upwards between the trees. It was an easy trail, but a sudden thought brought Jigme to a halt. He realised with some dismay that he had nothing to give this famous man and his wife as an offering. He knew it would be very rude to go empty handed.

He squatted down beside the path and emptied out his bag. There was the drawstring purse the magician had given him, his woollen hat, a silk offering scarf, a few pieces of meat and dried cheese, his water flask, his catapult, some dusty bits of paper with hard crusts of leftover bread in them and to his amazement there was also a bright red and yellow pomegranate. Where it could have come from he could not imagine. He sniffed it suspiciously. It was certainly quite real. Perhaps Lily had slipped it there when he was not looking.

He put it aside and opened the velvet purse. There was almost nothing left in it, but one small coin was particularly bright and new, and although he knew it was different from the money the people here used, he decided it would do and slipped it in his pocket. He was still dissatisfied however. He was not at all sure the fruit would not disappear again and felt he should really have something else to give as well. He looked around.

Further up the hill he could see there was a beautiful tree in flower, so packing up his things he scrambled up and picked one of the large, white blossoms. He put it carefully in his bag and continued on his way. As he walked he could feel the round hardness of the pomegranate bumping against his side. He wondered why he had not noticed it before. It was very odd.

After a while he came to a place where the hillside had been cut into terraces with rows of maize planted on them. Beyond was a thatched, red, mud farmhouse and as far as Jigme could see the path went no further. A woman was standing on the porch cleaning rice for the morning meal.

"Hello!" Jigme called out. "Is this the way to the arrow maker?"

The woman shook her head.

"No, you missed the turning. You should have taken the small left-hand path at the fork. There's no way up from here."

The boy began retracing his steps. He had not noticed a fork in the path at all. He had been thinking about the pomegranate. For a moment he saw Lily's face grinning at him and had the idea she had been distracting him on purpose.

After ten minutes or so he came to a place where indeed an alternative trail branched away in the other direction and soon he was above the woods and could see back over the valley. The view was wonderful. Jigme paused. A light mist still clung to the outskirts of the city and here and there temple pinnacles glittered golden in the early morning light. It looked like a magic, fairy kingdom.

It was only a little way to the top of the hill now. Jigme climbed up the last stretch and found himself on a wide grassy knoll. Not far off was a small hut and a couple were sitting in the open with a cooking fire close by. The woman was busy cutting vegetables and a long lean man was sitting so that Jigme could only see him from behind.

"Well, well. We have a visitor." Said the woman as the boy appeared from below.

"If it's that priest again with his books, tell him he's come on the wrong day."

"It's not at all. It's a wee lad with funny clothes on." The woman had a sweet face and as Jigme approached he could not guess what age she was. She might have been older than his mother, and then perhaps she was not much more than a girl.

"What a relief. That sounds more interesting."

Jigme took the white flower out of his bag and felt for the pomegranate. It was still there. If anything, it seemed to have grown bigger. The man was sitting on a deer skin, so he placed the blossom, the fruit and the shining coin on it at his feet and stood respectfully waiting for the man to look up.

The man was sifting through a pile of straight, fine sticks, smooth and rounded like reeds from a river. In the end he picked one out, examined it carefully and then handed it to Jigme.

"Here, take a look at this and tell me: is it straight or isn't it?"

All the sticks had looked straight to Jigme, so he thought this must be some kind of test, or maybe a trick. He held the stick at arms length, first vertically and then horizontally. It looked alright. Then he peered at it closely. The grain all seemed to be running in the same direction. His brother had shown him how to make a catapult from a forked branch like the one he had with him, so he knew a twisty stick was no good for anything much. He closed one eye and squinted along it. That seemed to be fine too. Finally he ran it gently between his finger and thumb, and he thought he felt a very slight imperfection. He scrutinised it minutely, but could see nothing. He turned it around and tried again and once more detected a single spot that was a touch uneven.

"Well?" asked the man. "How is it?"

Jigme was embarrassed. He was not sure if he was about to say something stupid or not.

"I think it's straight, but there's one place where it feels as if it's got a tiny lump inside, but I don't see anything."

"Good lad! Well done! I'm glad to see there's more than barley bran between your ears! Even an invisible flaw like that can send an arrow off course, no matter how well you aim." Then he added "I think that entitles you to share our breakfast," and he took the stick back again.

"Watch out!"

Jigme had stepped backwards and barely missed crunching underfoot a pile of radishes that were lying in the grass.

"Now don't let a simple compliment send you all of a heap or you'll destroy the meal before we can eat it! Sit down and keep those boots of yours out of trouble."

Jigme sat down on a small straw mat that the woman passed to him and watched as the arrowsmith went back to sorting through the pile of sticks. After a little he pushed them aside and unwrapped a cloth to reveal a selection of birds' feathers, which he proceeded to sort out according to size. There were long grey and white ones, shiny black ones and smaller brown ones. Some were flecked with colour.

There was something enormously attractive about the man's hands. They were old hands, strong and sinewy and clearly used to any kind of hard work. But the fingers were long and elegant and had a sensitivity that might well have befitted a painter or even a dancer. He lifted each feather with the greatest care, almost as if it were still part of a living creature. It was more like a caress of affection.

"I never cease to marvel at how beautifully they're made." He blew softly on the feather in his hand.

"The slightest change in a current of air and the delicate barbs along each side can shift to assist in flight – just enough give and just enough resistance.

Have you ever seen a mountain hawk swoop down to kill its prey? Imagine how perfectly aligned each detail of its plumage must be for it to gauge and trust in the accuracy of its fall."

He lifted the feather and stroked the air with it, watching the way its edges lifted as he did so.

"So what brings you here to see me?" he asked, moving the feather this way and that.

Jigme explained about his mother, his journey and how the Baba and Lily had suggested he find the arrow makers. The woman laughed when he mentioned Lily.

"So you've met my little sister. Did she behave herself?"

Jigme was not sure what to say, but his hesitation was enough.

"Ah! I see she took every opportunity she could to tease you. I don't suppose she often gets a visitor like you."

She reached for the radishes and began slicing them and putting them in the cooking pot.

"Well, what exactly do you think I am?" asked the man.

He was riffling through a cloth bag and eventually produced a small knife.

"An arrow maker," Jigme replied.

"Yes, but besides that. Carpenters and blacksmiths aren't usually doctors too."

Jigme thought a moment. The man was sharpening the knife on a flat black stone.

"A magician, maybe?"

The corners of the man's mouth twitched slightly.

"Pfuff! I turn you into a bat!"

With lightening speed, he had turned round and was pointing the knife handle at Jigme's nose. The boy nearly leaped out of his skin. In panic he looked down at his hands. The very tips of his fingers were turning black and slowly sprouting tiny little curved claws. He blinked in horror, and the vision was gone. He inspected them nervously. Yes they still looked human enough. His fear slowly subsided, but the arrowsmith was looking at him very fiercely indeed.

"If you think I'm a wizard you're horribly trusting."

He went back to sharpening the blade.

"Don't you know magic tricks are often the only thing magicians do know how to do? They'll catch your interest with some cunning piece of shape-shifting and delusion and make you lose your mind. And that's not an easy thing to find again. Once you're hooked they can lead you around by the nose for years, making you do all kinds of foolish and wicked things for them. All power games and no human kindness. Very dangerous!"

Jigme thought about this for a while.

"Yes, but you're a yogi too."

The arrowsmith's wife came out with a noise half chortle, half snort, and banged her ladle on the side of the pot.

"Yogis, bogies!" she said irreverently. "I was living with a yogi once," she slyly shifted her eyes sideways, "not naming any names, of course, and just as I was serving lunch he went into a deep meditative trance. Well, rather than let all the food go to waste, I fed his half to a starving, pregnant cat that was living in the woods nearby."

"A long, long time passed. Many moons waxed and waned and one day the trance fell away and the yogi emerged from meditation into the material world again. And do you know what the first thing he said was? "Where's my radish curry?""

The woman shook with a peel of laughter.

"I said to him: "My dear! You're joking of course. It saved a mother cat's life and a whole generation of kittens has been born, grown old and died on the strength of that curry. What on earth was the point of such profound austerity and meditation if you are still completely attached to who you are, where you think you are and what you thought was going on? Quite a waste of time don't you think? There's more to being a realised yogi than that." And he had to agree."

She laughed.

"So now, even though that was years ago, I make him radish curry once a month, just to remind him. And today's the day!"

"It's all true," said the arrow maker ruefully and smiled.

"Conceit and self-deception are a yogi's curse. If he's lucky he has someone with clear vision and a warm heart to point it out to him. Otherwise it's just the blind leading the sightless; out of the snake-pit and straight down the well."

He very carefully started cutting the feather into crosswise sections and laying the pieces out on the edge of his deerskin. Then he selected a shaft from the pile and deftly cut notches in its end. He took a long time fitting the pieces of feather into the notches, feeling the balance and then readjusting them. Finally satisfied, he stood the shaft upright in a pot and put his knife away. He looked up at Jigme.

"We can make the arrow, but you must make the bow and aim it right."

Jigme wondered what he meant, but before he could ask, the arrowsmith's wife intervened.

"The food's ready. Perhaps you could go to the hut and get some dishes for me."

Jigme did as he was asked.

The food was delicious. In a way he was not surprised a memory of it had lingered on in the recesses of the yogi's mind, and when he was offered a second helping, Jigme accepted eagerly.

When everything had been cleared away the arrowsmith collected a large curved knife in a leather scabbard from the hut and called Jigme to him.

"We're going into the forest, you and I. Your job will be to find a length of wood to make yourself a bow. Come!"

They set off across the hill and soon came to an area thickly overgrown with trees.

"What you need is a piece that's strong, straight and pliable. It mustn't bend too easily though and should snap back straight as soon as you release it. You need a piece a couple of hands longer than your outstretched arms. It's no good if it has twigs branching off it, nor must it be a piece of this year's growth. You must cut it away with a single slice. And take care! The knife is very sharp."

They came to a clearing and the man gave the boy the knife.

"Tuck this in your belt, and before you make a cut, ask the tree for permission. They have feelings too, you know. You can make your own way back. I have to go higher up."

And he set off through the trees and disappeared.

Jigme turned around and surveyed the trees that surrounded the clearing. There were clearly a number of different varieties. There did not seem to be any willows which, because they grew near his home, were the only kind he knew well. He approached one tree and looked up into its foliage. It was a strong tree with thick, dark bark and fat branches. He could see at once that it would not be any good for his purpose. No branch reached the length he needed without forking first. He moved on to another one. This one was also no good because although the branches grew for quite a length without dividing, none of them were straight. They seem to have grown in short spurts before deciding to change direction, as if avoiding all kinds of invisible obstacles.

Jigme did not really get to consider the next tree because when he looked up he found a very large bull monkey sitting just above his head. It was absorbed in preening its fur and bared its teeth with such annoyance at being disturbed that Jigme decided to leave him well alone.

The next tree had branches that were far too delicate, and the one after that was so rigid that the whole trunk seemed in danger of cracking when he tried tugging at one of its limbs. He began to realise that his task was not going to be easy. He had wandered away from the clearing now. There were trees with berries and trees with leaves like hands. Some were short and fat and some were slender and slightly droopy. Some were graceful with feathery foliage that shivered in the breeze, some were tough and prickly, but none of them seemed to suit the arrowsmith's requirements.

After a little he sat down on a tree-stump to take a rest. It was pleasant in the wood, fresh and quiet and very green. His presence disturbed the courtship of two butterflies on a bush nearby and sent them skittering off in a flash of orange. He took the knife out of his belt and removed it carefully from its scabbard. It was quite heavy, with a wooden handle and a large blade that jutted out at an angle. He tested the cutting edge with his thumb and immediately a fine line appeared oozing drops of blood. It was certainly very sharp indeed. He sucked the small wound for a moment and looked at the knife with renewed respect. Then grasping it cautiously with his right hand he sliced at the edge of the dead stump he was sitting on. A neat, triangular chip of wood flew into the air and landed several feet away. The knife would make a formidable weapon in a time of need. He slid it back into its sheath out of harm's way.

He stood up and began heading north, scanning the trees as he went. After a while the hillside revealed a long, deep, wooded cleft. It was much colder there as if the sun hardly ever reached the recesses of that part of the forest. There was less grass underfoot and the ground became harsh and rocky. Jigme picked his way upwards. He was suddenly struck by the sight, not far away, of a tree that was completely different from all the rest. It was standing alone on the side

72

of a steep drop. It was clearly very old. A part of it seemed to be dead already, although some of its branches were still covered in dark, green leaves, small and pointed and very thin. He picked his way towards it carefully and stopped on a boulder in front of it where he could examine its branches.

It looked perfect. He reached up and caught hold of one of its dead limbs. It was strong and still springy, and he knew without doubt this was the tree he had been searching for. The main trunk impressed him by how ancient, resilient and friendly it looked. It was wrinkled and very twisted. It reminded him of his great-grandfather who had lived with them until he had died a few years back. He had been the strongest man in the village – so everyone said.

It pleased him too that he would be able to take what he wanted from a part that was no longer alive. He supposed it would not hurt the tree when he cut it, but he thought he had better ask it first. He brushed aside a feeling of foolishness and stood up straight.

"My name is Jigme and I come from Tibet. Please can I cut down one of your dead branches to make bow?"

There was absolute silence. He had not been told whether to expect an answer so he waited without moving to see what would happen. It was then that he became aware that a single shaft of sunlight had somehow penetrated the thickly covered slopes above and fell in a small bright pool on the stricken side of the ancient tree.

He took the knife out, carefully measured the length he needed on one of the branches and hacked at it close to the trunk. The knife was so sharp that a single stroke was all it took to sever it, and it fell instantly at his feet.

"Thank you." he said.

He picked the piece of wood up and pared off the end where it divided into several dry twigs. He was about to strip the bark off too, but decided there might be a special way to do that, and set off instead the way he had come with the branch over his shoulder.

When he returned to the place where the arrowsmith lived, the woman was busy working a small piece of metal with a slender file. Jigme crouched down beside her.

"What are you doing?" he asked.

"I'm making the arrow head for you." Then seeing the look of surprise on Jigme's face she added, "I learned to make them from my father when I was a child. He taught me how to combine the perfect metals and how to create the ideal shape with them."

She continued working as she talked.

"Perfect balance is even more important in the arrow's tip than in the shaft. It carries the weight of your concentration straight to the target you're aiming at. My father was once forced to make some arrows for a very wicked man – he had no choice. So by an invisible twist in the arrow's core we ensured the villain could never shoot straight. And he never found out why."

She laughed.

"We can be quite cunning if we have to!"

Later on the arrowsmith returned with a bundle of firewood. He looked at Jigme.

"How did you do then?" he asked.

Jigme showed him the branch he had brought.

"Ah! I see you found my old friend. I thought you might. He's the only one in the forest with anything worth having for this job."

He looked the piece of wood over.

"You must remove the bark carefully without damaging the smooth layer underneath. Here, you'd better use this knife," he said producing a small bone-handled implement from his pocket, "that other one will be too heavy and hard to control."

Jigme sat down cross-legged and began his task. Even with a small blade it was not as easy as it looked. In some places the outer sheath was already dried out and came away easily. In others it was still adhering quite strongly to the wood beneath and it was almost impossible not to make gashes in it. He tried to be slow and painstaking, but he felt he was not doing very well.

Half way along as he lifted away one strip of bark he disturbed a minute, beetle-like creature who obviously thought it had found a secure home for itself. The tiny thing was truly furious. It reared up and gave an unmistakable hiss at Jigme's hand. The boy was astonished. He plucked a long stem of grass and poked the insect in the chest. Again it turned to face its aggressor and uttered an audibly defiant noise. Jigme lifted the branch up to look more closely. It was a terribly ugly looking little bug. He supposed that to something its own size it must look quite fearsome. He was about to poke it again when he remembered the demon of the crag, and how frightened he had been himself. Considering

74

how gigantic and alien he must seem to this beetle, it was showing quite extraordinary fearlessness. It occurred to him that perhaps it was not fair to tease such courage, so he let it walk up the grass stem instead and placed it among some leaves where it would not get stepped on.

Stripping the wood for the bow was taking such a long time that the arrowsmith ended up finishing it off for him. Apart from one or two spots where Jigme's knife had slipped it looked smooth and shiny when it was done. The arrowsmith oiled it and rounded the ends off and then together they arched it over and fixed the string in place. It made a wonderfully musical note when it was plucked.

In the meantime the woman had done the final polishing that gave the arrowhead its perfect point and had attached it in place at the end of the shaft.

"Let's see you shoot it now," the arrowsmith said.

They set up a wooden plate as a target on a tree at the end of the knoll. Then he showed Jigme how to stand and how to hold the bow.

The boy's first shot was extraordinarily accurate.

"Try again!" the man told him.

Feeling elated Jigme collected the arrow and let it fly once more. This time it went a long way off course. He tried again. It fell too short. He tried again and again and then many times more, but he could not repeat his original success. Once the arrow flew far off into the bushes and it was a while before he could find it again. He became increasingly cross and frustrated and his shoulders grew tired. The arrowsmith had turned his attention elsewhere and had wandered off into the hut. His wife remained watching Jigme's fruitless efforts.

Eventually she called out to him.

"That's enough! You'd better stop for a moment. You'll only wear yourself out like that."

She stood up and walked over to him. She took the bow and arrow from him and made him stand back.

"Watch."

She swept the hair out of her eyes and took aim. Lightly, gracefully, easily and with a smile on her face she let the arrow fly, and, as if it had nowhere else to go, it sped through the air and with a gentle thud it struck the mark precisely.

Jigme could not keep himself from clapping, it was so perfectly done. The woman laughed.

"Alright, you give it one more go now and I'll try and tell you how to do it."

She handed the bow back to him and he went to retrieve the arrow. Then he took up his position where she had been standing and took a deep breath.

"Good," said the arrowsmith's wife. "Now listen" and she began to recite in a sing-song voice:

"Empty your thoughts, the moment's now and here.
Be wide awake, banish all doubts and fear.
Plant your feet firmly, lift the bow up straight.
Fix the goal fast, your gaze controls your fate.
Embrace the target with your heart. Relax your mind.
Stretch without straining and be wise and kind.
Feel the wood singing softly in your grip,
Don't let attention waver, nor your finger slip.
The arrow's flight is yours alone to choose,
Knowing the world is one you cannot lose."

As she chanted Jigme felt himself somehow taken over by a much larger vision of things. He had the strange idea that if he wanted to he could reach out his hand and touch the target with no trouble at all. As her last words fell into silence he took no more than another second to feel comfortable with his aim and then released the string. The arrow shot across the hillside and hit the plate with such a terrifying "thwack!" that it split the wood from top to bottom.

There was silence and Jigme viewed his work for a moment with amazed satisfaction. Then it occurred to him that his instructors might not be so pleased. Feeling a little abashed, he turned round to find the woman with her hand over her mouth as if to hide a grin, and the arrowsmith beside her looking at him rather severely.

"You don't need a boulder to crack a walnut, you know. I think that was exaggerating a bit. But you seem to have got the point!"

They returned to their places near the fire and the arrowsmith gave Jigme a narrow bamboo tube with a thong for a handle to put his arrow in and an orange, cloth bag for his bow. It seemed that all that was left was for Jigme to find out what he was going to have to use them for.

"Tonight I shall climb up onto a high ridge with you and show you a cave where you can sleep. Tomorrow you must walk for a couple of hours beyond the tree line until you come to a monument covered with prayer flags and bearing a crescent moon on its pinnacle. I can't say how long you will have to wait there, but eventually something looking like a very strange bird will appear in the sky. As soon as it is within range you must take aim and shoot to kill it. Don't hesitate. Don't miss. You won't get a second chance and you only have one arrow."

Jigme suddenly felt chill as if the sun had ducked behind a cloud. He could sense his skin contracting into goose pimples. He had not really considered that he might have to use the weapon to actually kill something. Perhaps it should have been obvious to him from the beginning. He wondered what would happen if he failed and if the bird-creature would kill him instead. All the target practice had been child's play compared with this.

He thought of the story of the hunter and hoped he was not being asked to bring death to something innocent and harmless. He could not imagine this couple telling him to do something like that but he felt confused even so. He tried to quell a surge of anxiety. Looking round he realised the arrowsmith's wife was watching him with some concern. The look in her eyes reminded him so much of his mother he was tempted to bury his head in her lap just to feel her protective warmth.

She leaned over and touched him gently on the knee.

"Don't be afraid," she said, "everything will be alright."

That night, as soon as the moon was up, Jigme and the arrowsmith set off through the forest. It was quite difficult at first picking one's way up the steep trail. The ground was patterned with dark pools of shadow and bright stripes of moonlight. Rough places looked deceptively white and smooth, and the black places concealed all kinds of treacherous pitfalls. Jigme found himself tripping and stumbling like a drunkard, while his long-legged guide was as lithe and nimble as a cat and continually had to wait for him to catch up.

It was several hours before they were out of the trees and making their way across a pale, moonlit landscape of shrubs and grass and boulders. Higher up they crossed a ridge and not far down the other side was a small cavern with a sandy floor covered with twigs and soft dried foliage. There was just enough room for one person to lie comfortably in its shadow and still have a view of the milky hills around.

The arrowsmith made sure Jigme was going to be alright alone there and then gave him his final instructions.

"When it's all over, leave the bow and arrow behind the carved stones on a cairn near the monument. Like that they will find their way back to me. You won't need them again."

Then, wishing Jigme good luck, he turned and strode away across the mountain, swiftly disappearing over the ridge and into the night.

Jigme was exhausted and slept almost at once, but later, as the night progressed, his slumber was overtaken by a vivid dream. The boy found himself at home in his village. It was the day of the annual fair. Everyone was preparing for the yak racing and archery contests on horseback and there was an air of great excitement and festivity. Today there was to be a special contest and Jigme was to take part with his new bow and arrow.

A target with a juniper wreath around it had been set up on a pole in a long courtyard. Crowds of spectators had gathered around and Jigme discovered it was his turn to show his skill, although he had not noticed any other competitors. He tried to remember the instructions he had been given, raised his bow and took aim.

Just as he was about to release the string, to his astonishment the target transformed itself into a rainbow-coloured fish that was dangling from a line. A metal hook had caught it through the lower lip and it was eying him mournfully and gasping for air. Jigme hesitated and tried to collect himself, but in another moment it had changed again, this time into the talking frog that had helped him across the lake. The frog was shaking its head from side to side in what seemed to be a disapproving and dejected manner.

Jigme held fast to the bowstring, keeping the arrow in check, but becoming increasingly disconcerted. It was only a moment before the frog too vanished and in its place was the cliff-top tiger. Its dried skin was hanging limply on the pole, but its living head was pushed through the juniper wreath and it was snarling and struggling fruitlessly as if caught by the neck in a trap. It did not seem aware of Jigme at all.

Jigme blinked hard. The crowd around him was getting impatient and his arms were beginning to ache. He was afraid the pressure on his fingers was so great they would release the arrow whether he wanted to or not. He tried to focus on what was really there and found he was aiming at a small boy, bound hand and foot to the pole. It was the son of his next-door-neighbour. He had known him almost all his life. There were tears pouring down his pointed, little face, and he was looking at Jigme in desperation.

Jigme felt himself beginning to tremble. Drops of sweat were forming on his forehead. By now several of the spectators were jeering at him and calling him a coward. He could hear mocking laughter and grumbles of dissatisfaction all around him. He closed his eyes and tried to clear his mind. Then summoning all his strength, he straightened his back and poised himself to shoot. He looked once more at the target. But the pole with the juniper target had gone.

The courtyard stretched before him, yellow and dusty in the sunshine. Twenty feet or so in front of him was a woman. Her back was towards him and her arms were raised as she pinned her long, dark braids up on top of her head. The silky material of her blouse fell in folds around her elbows, reflecting the golden morning light and revealing the wide conch bracelets on her wrists. A familiar bunch of keys hung glinting from her belt. It was his mother.

"No! No!"

With whatever remaining energy he had, he flung the bow, arrow and all, to the ground and in agonised defeat collapsed beside them. He felt stupid and muddled and humiliated – not to mention exhausted. He covered his head with his arms and pressed his nose into the dirt, wishing himself a thousand miles away. Everything had become too complicated. He had had enough. He huddled there, his mind spinning and his heart thumping inside his ribs.

Little by little, profound, empty darkness began to envelope him, pulling and pressing him down. The harsh voices of the crowd seemed to be drifting away from him, until they faded altogether and an eerie silence settled. It was with some curiosity that he realised his wish had somehow been answered. He was in fact quite alone and far, far from his village. There was nothing but thick blackness all around him and his breath was coming in short, painful gulps. For some time it did not occur to him to roll over and open his eyes, but when he did, he found he was back in the cave again.

The moon was shining in his face and he was damp with perspiration. The bright, silvery light dazzled him. As he lay there panting he tried to make sense of the shapes around him. The orange bag containing the bow and the bamboo quiver were propped against the wall next to him, where he had left them. His boots lay discarded on the floor.

His eyes travelled across the leaf-strewn ground, patterned with moonlight and shadows, then stopped. Near the opening to the cave they had come across a pair of feet. They were quite small, pale, bare feet, but there was no doubt that was what they were. Cautiously he looked up and found the arrowsmith's wife standing against the rocky wall looking at him. She was dressed in a long, red shawl and her hair hung loose over her shoulders. The brightness of the night gave her skin a strange and beautiful iridescence. She smiled when she saw him looking at her and crouched down beside him.

"A jealous spirit from the forest followed you here and was trying to make you ill. Here, let me put this on you for protection."

Jigme raised his head and she tied a thread with something hanging on it around his neck.

"Now go back to sleep again," she said, and she ran her hand gently over his face and closed his eyes.

Jigme could see the stone monument covered in prayer flags from quite a long way off, but it was almost midday before he reached it. He had noticed there seemed to be quite a lot of movement around it besides the multicoloured banners flapping in the breeze, but it was not until he was on a level with it that he could see what was there.

The hill-top was occupied by a group of very odd-looking birds. He had certainly never seen anything like them before. One black one with a curved pink beak and an impressive shiny crest was walking up and down as if on sentry duty. It waddled slightly from left to right as it went and as Jigme approached it paused in mid-stride and observed him imperiously with its head cocked sideways.

Another brown one was busily inspecting the cracks between the flagstones and making a fussy quacking noise as it went. It took no notice of the approaching boy. Jigme supposed it was hunting for something to eat in the dirt, but it did not seem to be having much luck.

Other birds were swooping out of the sky and crash-landing on the grass verge, then taking off again. They seemed to be having a lot of fun. As soon as they spotted Jigme a couple of them changed course and skimmed one after the other over his head, coming so close he felt his hair lift as they passed.

None of them looked in the least ominous and he felt sure he was not supposed to shoot any of them, but he took out his bow and arrow in readiness. He circumambulated the white, stone monument and waited to see what would happen.

For a while he squatted happily in the sunshine and then, remembering his dream of the night before, he felt around his neck to see if the arrowsmith's wife had really put something there. And indeed she had. Caught underneath his collar was what felt like a piece of cord, and peering down he discovered he was wearing a thick, red thread. Attached to it was a tiny, pointed object. It was difficult to see what it was at first, but squinting down his nose and tucking in his chin he could just make out it was a little wooden dagger. It seemed to have a triangular, three-sided blade and some kind of animal's head on the handle. It felt very smooth and warm to his fingertips, as if it had been worn by many people before him. He tucked it back inside his shirt to keep it safe and felt very comforted knowing it was there.

Time passed and the sun made Jigme drowsy. He was just in the middle of a yawn when a shadow fell across the ground in front of him and made him look up. Something very large and dark had appeared in the sky. It had broad, strong wings and was getting closer with every second. Jigme was wide awake in a moment and grabbed his bow.

As he got to his feet and stood ready he felt both excited and suddenly peculiarly blood-thirsty. He gazed upwards and took aim. He thought of the arrowsmith and his wife, tried to sweep all sensations and emotions from his mind and pulled back the string. Clear, cool air filled his lungs. The bow and arrow hummed with tautness in his fingers. Then, praying there was no mistake and that only good would come of it, he let go and sent the feathered shaft flying up, up into the air. Clean and straight it vanished into the heart of the dark shape, and whatever it was began to float gently down to earth.

Jigme stood back and shaded his eyes against the sunlight. He watched the object falling slowly down.

"Smack on target, I'd say," said a voice at last and there, hovering a few feet above the ground he could see the form was a very strange kind of airborne creature.

It was clutching the arrow in one hand and seemed to be neither bird nor man, but something in between. It had clawed feet, a bird-like face with a dangerous-looking, hooked beak, smooth, broad, red shoulders and arms, and a powerful pair of blue-green wings. It looked cheerful and thoroughly unruffled.

"As you can see, I'm neither this nor that. So there was never really any chance you could harm me! If you'd been bent on destroying me as a thing you'd have been way off the mark. Then I might have been obliged to swoop down and perform some nasty kind of dramatics. But as it was you got it exactly right. So here we are."

It perched itself on the side of the monument and smoothed back its feathers.

"Let me introduce myself. I'm the red Garuda. I'm pretty sure I know what you're here for, but you'd better tell me yourself, just so we get things straight."

Once more Jigme told his tale. The other birds had gathered at Garuda's feet and listened with varying degrees of attentiveness. Garuda himself rocked gently backwards and forwards with his eyes half closed, making occasional clicking noises with his beak. When Jigme had finished he looked at him thoughtfully for a moment with his head on one side. Then he spoke.

"It's all a question of balance."

He gesticulated airily at the scene and its surroundings.

"Everything here is made up of earth, air, fire, water and space – even ourselves. For survival the mix has to be just right. A trout and its spawn, whose natural home is the river, if beached on dry land, will lose their magical fishiness in no time. They'll just become dust of the earth instead."

"It's the same with an eagle's egg. Until it's had just the right amount of heat for the right amount of time, the little bird within will never finally have the form and energy to peck its way into the airy world."

He folded his arms across his chest.

"But then too much heat and we'd all be roast turkeys."

From the corner of his eye Jigme noticed that one of the smaller birds winced at this last remark and moved a little closer to the group

"On the whole, once we're here though, most wild creatures know by instinct exactly which substances will do them good and keep their motors running. Take me, for example. Settle for the wrong diet and I'll either be fat and sweaty, lying around in my eyrie, too heavy and confused even to move, or else too weak and wistful. Then when it's time for lift off...... Not a chance."

"But human beings? Tsk. Tsk."

He clicked his beak in disapproval.

"They do get carried away sometimes:

> Nut crunch, eggplant, meat loaf, paw-paw,
> Cocoa, cabbage, kumquat, coleslaw,
> Rutabaga, oxtail, salmon,
> Slice of whole-wheat bread with jam on,
> Goose gazpacho, toddy truffle,
> Prune cake, pretzel, puffball, waffle,
> Swordfish steak with Burmese sago,
> Muffin, herring, guava, gumbo,
> Spotted dick and Windsor soup,
> Chilled honeydew or cantaloupe,
> Turkey giblets, flapjack, fondue,
> Elderberry wine and lamb stew,
> Chowder, fritter, Roquefort rarebit,
> Sherbet, quiche, king prawn in aspic.
> You won't know until you've tasted
> If it's better fried or basted,
> Pickled, devilled, baked or roasted,
> Marinated, hung or toasted.
> Breakfast, dinner, lunch and tea,
> How delicious they can be!
> Eighty-four thousand things to eat
> Make every day a special treat."

The Garuda let out a great squawk of mirth and was joined in a cacophony of honking and cackling by his bird audience.

85

"It's a terrible temptation I can see that. But oh, my tail feathers! No wonder humans come in such funny shapes and sizes... not to mention the complicated illnesses they get."

The thought seemed to sober him and regaining his poise he pointed a wingtip at Jigme.

"Can you imagine, far, far, away across the sea there's a man who's so fat he can't get out of bed. He's been lying there wolfing down meal after meal for so long that he's become a giant fleshy hillock. If ever he did want to get up and go for a walk, his family would have to remove the house brick by brick around him to get him out."

"And then, in the same land, there are other people who are so afraid of being called plump or portly that they hardly eat at all. Their bodies are like skeletons. All that's left of them is a harsh wind that blows their minds this way and that. Not only so, but with it comes a sweet, beguiling voice that tells them how beautiful they'd be if they were even just a little smaller. It's so sad."

Garuda performed an elegant arabesque, first on one foot and then on the other.

"Harmony and balance," he said. "If you get it right you have the best chance of skimming your way through this life and accomplishing all kinds of interesting and useful things."

He pirouetted.

"Of course, you can't always avoid diseases, obstacles, disasters – no one can. But, like I said, it's all a question of earth, fire, water, air and space all dancing with each other. That's what you and I and everything else are made of, each in our different proportions. So, if you know what's what, there's no substance at all that can't be used as a medicine for one purpose or another."

He paused a moment in thought.

"But I don't pretend it's easy. We're slaves to our likes and dislikes; do like hummingbirds, don't like vultures. We cling to this and reject that. And the more we stick to what pleases us and avoid what doesn't, the less we can see the subtle qualities of things. And sooner or later – clang, bang – as sure as ducks lay eggs, our mind and body get hopelessly out of balance."

The Garuda pretended to stagger along the edge of the monument as if a fierce gale was blowing instead of the light breeze that tugged at the prayer flags. Reaching a corner he made as if to trip, flailed his arms and wings backwards in mock panic, fell sideways and then, catching himself just before he hit the ground, swooped gracefully back to perch on his spot one more.

The black crested bird with the pink beak gave a shrill whistle of admiration. Jigme jumped. While the Garuda had been talking, he had been mesmerised by the creature's feathers, which had taken on a flickering quality like layers of shimmering flames. He blinked and sniffed the mountain air to try and regain a feeling of his own solidity.

Noticing the boy was at something of a loss the Garuda leaned forward and tapped him gently with the arrow.

"All a bit much isn't it? My profound apologies. Lets get down to the grit and gravel; how to help your mother."

Straightening back up he tucked the arrow in his armpit, folded his arms and drummed the fingers of his right hand on his left elbow for a moment. He turned his head slightly from side to side.

"I have a hunch," he said at last, " - and you can usually trust a Garuda's hunch – that it's the water element. It's a matter of a watery disorder I would say. And that might not mean a great deal to you, but at least it points out where you have to go next. Do you have a hat?"

Surprised, Jigme nodded.

"Let's see it."

Jigme collected his shoulder-bag from the grass verge where he had left it and pulled out his woollen cap, dusting it free of crumbs and fragments of dried cheese. The Garuda inspected it.

"Yes," he said "that's just the thing. Now wait there a moment."

He flew off to a nearby rock and planted himself on top with his feet wide apart and his claws gripping the edge on either side. Then, after shaking himself a little, he spread out his wings and arced them high above his head. Again there seemed to be a ripple across his plumage, as if a line of fire was igniting its outer tips. Left, right and behind he made a quick, fierce movement with his beak, striking once at each wing and once at his tail.

Three golden-tipped feathers spun upwards into the air, were lifted for a moment on the breeze and then spiralled onto the rock at the Garuda's feet. He examined them carefully, picked them up and flew back to perch beside Jigme once again.

"You're going to have to visit the king of the naga-serpents," he said. "Since time immemorial Garudas are the only living things to have power over them. They have little trust or respect for human beings. They consider them a careless, greedy lot, who cause damage everywhere they go. But just as the nagas are lords of the jewelled waters within the earth, they know we Garudas are emperors of the skies above them. They need rain from the heavens and they have no desire to have us as their enemies."

"In order for them to take you seriously it must be clear to them that you were sent by me. In fact, they have to spot it straight away. So you must fix these feathers on your hat and that way the moment they set eyes on you they'll know who's on your side. You'd better do it now."

Jigme took the feathers from him. He poked them through the weave of the material on top and bound the ends tightly underneath with a few loose strands of wool.

"Now, when you put it on, you mustn't think "Here's my old hat with a bit of bird's tail in it." You must know that it's your ceremonial crown. You must wear it with dignity and hold your head high. The moment it's on your head you are my regent and you must behave appropriately. Treating the nagas with courtesy will definitely further your cause. And for goodness sake don't step on any of them."

Jigme liked the way the hat looked with the feathers stuck in it. It had a rather stylish air. He turned it inside out so the plumes would be protected and put it carefully inside his bag.

"Where do I have to go to find the King of the Nagas? Where does he live?"

Jigme hoped he was not going to have to venture into any underground labyrinths. He had never much liked dark, confined spaces and not surprisingly the idea of feeling his way along damp, unlit passages full of snakes terrified him.

The Garuda saw the look on his face and gave a cheerful squawk.

"My dear, little friend, I wouldn't dream of sending you off to find the Nagaraja's palace. For one thing it's way down deep in the earth and it would take you weeks to get there. Secondly, only a very great yogi indeed could overcome the poisonous obstacles and terrifying protectors that guard the serpent's treasure land. Many people have tried, and almost no one has come back alive."

He shook his head.

"No, at this time of the year the king has a favourite watering hole that he likes to visit with his entourage. It's in a cool and peaceful spot at the eastern end of the sacred valley. Only the local farmers know he goes there, and they try to make sure he enjoys his recreation there undisturbed as his presence ensures there will be enough water to irrigate the crops."

"Dawn and dusk are the times nagas like the best. They especially enjoy bathing in that bluish-grey twilight that is neither night nor day, but something magic and in between. That's probably the best time for you to try and meet him."

Jigme felt reassured, and even somewhat excited. He had heard stories of the King of the Nagas, the fabled custodian of countless riches hidden beneath the surface of the earth. Jigme knew that wherever there were buried gems, or treasures lying deep down in mountain lakes, the naga-guardians would be keeping a watchful eye. He also knew they could summon fearsome rainstorms and crippling droughts if so inclined, and it was very foolish to treat them disrespectfully. He had never imagined he might one day meet the Nagaraj himself.

"I have nothing to give him as a gift," said Jigme.

He thought for a moment.

"Well I still have a white, silk scarf, though it might be a bit screwed up. Will that do? Do you think it's enough?"

The Garuda smiled, his cheeks crinkling on either side of his beak.

"I think that would be just fine. Let's see if we can smooth it out a bit first though."

Jigme extracted it from the bottom of his bag and the Garuda took hold of one end in his beak, while Jigme held on to the other. The wind whipped at its creases, and a few dusty crumbs of dried cheese scattered down onto the flagstones where an interested bird gobbled them up.

Between the two of them they managed to make it look a little more presentable. Jigme folded it carefully and tucked it into his coat pocket. Then the Garuda returned the arrow to him.

"Here, you'd better take care of this. Then I think we'll have to try a little trick to get you back to the valley before evening falls. What do you think?"

The Garuda closed one eye and fixed the other on Jigme with an enquiring gleam.

The boy was not at all sure he wanted any more tricks. A part of him longed for a very ordinary day – a day with no surprises and no peculiar twists. He wished he could just sit on his own doorstep for the afternoon with little Leo for company. He sighed inwardly and thought how glad he was that Leo had never started talking like a human and giving him good advice. Then feeling he was being ungrateful to all the different kinds of people and creatures who had been helping him, he busied himself looking around for his belongings. He really did not want to be rude, and tried to give the impression he was ready for anything

He put the bow back in its bag. Then as he was fitting the arrow into its bamboo quiver he recalled that he was supposed to leave them hidden somewhere behind some stones. Scattered around the hilltop there were quite a number of piles of rocks, some left by pilgrims and some marking the trail running north. They all looked far too windswept and exposed to conceal anything. Even the grass was short and somewhat sparse, providing very little cover at all.

The Garuda had turned away and was busy conversing with the other birds. Jigme took a walk around the monument to see if there was anything suitable on the other side. Standing on a bluff he could make out a larger cairn a short way off the track, and as he approached it he could see it was surrounded by a circle of carved stone slabs. He was sure this had to be the arrowsmith's hiding place.

 Some of the stones had invocations and prayers engraved on them. Others bore magical syllables. Jigme picked his way slowly round the pile inspecting them. Here and there they were decorated with border designs and small pictures of animals. But one he found was quite different from the rest. For one thing it seemed much older than the others. Time and winter winds had softened the outlines and lichen had grown across the surface and filled in the gaps with patterns like greenish-yellow rosettes.

Jigme squatted on his haunches to look more closely at the carving and found it was a picture of a bearded man, sitting with his legs half-crossed and wearing boots something like his own. Picking dirt out of the cracks, Jigme followed the outlines of the body, which seemed to be dressed in a loose ornamental robe. He cleaned off the face and head to reveal a hat. It was also very similar to his own, though perhaps it was a little more regal. And as he brushed away the last fragments of grit he saw that it had, very clearly, a feather sticking out of the top of it.

Confident he had found the right spot he wiped the dirt off his hands and then carefully tucked the bow and arrow behind the stones, making sure no part of them was visible to an ordinary passer-by. He felt quite pleased with himself and for a moment wondered if the image was not smiling at him.

He could hear the birds whooping and carolling together and made his way back to join them. They seemed to be exchanging jokes with each other, though he could not understand what they were saying. Eventually the Garuda broke away and fixed his attention on Jigme once more.

"Right!" he said, "Are you ready for the next stage?"

Jigme smiled and nodded.

"Good! Then let's go over there."

He flicked a wing towards a clear, flat spot of grass on the far side of the hill.

"Perfect. Now sit down cross legged."

Jigme did as he was told.

"Put your hat on and make sure the feathers are standing upright. Yes, perfect. Now stretch out your arms and let the backs of your hands rest on your knees. Uh huh. Now curl your thumbs over – so. Bravo! Keep your back straight and your chin a little tucked in. Just hold that position and don't wriggle about."

The Garuda then stood directly in front of Jigme and began preening his wings with his beak. Then he tweaked at his long crest and ran his fingers through it so that it flowed back over his head. Jigme had not noticed before but in fact it was really rather like a mane.

"Now, start breathing so that the air goes all the way down to the pit of your belly – long, slow breaths in and out like this."

With each intake of air the bird almost seemed to double in size, though it might merely have been his feathers fluffing up. Jigme tried to copy him. For the first few minutes it seemed quite simple, but after that it began to get more difficult to sustain.

The concentration made him feel like he was wielding a large pair of bellows, or perhaps that he had turned into a pair of bellows himself. In and out, in and out; he wondered what would happen if he stopped. He had the horrible feeling he had forgotten how to breathe without thinking. His body had been happily inhaling and expelling air all his life and, now that he had tampered with its natural, unconscious rhythm, he felt he was doomed. In and out; he could feel the hair on the crown of his head start to prickle and a queasy panic stirring in his stomach.

"Relax! Let go!"

He heard the Garuda give a wonderful, liquid laugh that started like a mynah bird, corkscrewed and rippled like a nightingale, fell down a scale of half-a-dozen notes and landed in a deep soothing cooing like a wood pigeon.

"Don't try so hard."

Jigme shook himself and tried again. After a little he found himself falling into a comfortable rhythm as if his whole being was floating along on a current of air. He watched the Garuda who was standing arms outstretched and wings unfurled so that they formed a kind of archway over his head. It looked as if he was beginning to give off a warm, iridescent glow, and again Jigme noticed a shimmer of energy like fire or lightning high-lighting the tip of each feather.

"Picture yourself standing in front of a stone water-spout." Jigme closed his eyes and instantly his field of vision became intensely blue. Although he knew his eyes were shut, he had the feeling they were wide open. He gazed into the blueness and felt it settling all around him as if it stretched infinitely in all directions. The more he watched, the more he noticed it glimmered with uncountable rainbow particles floating and circling like dust in sunlight, and yet somehow the blue was unquestionably a glorious blue.

He was not sure he had ever seen a stone water-spout up close. He wondered what it was supposed to look like. He tried to imagine a mountain spring coming out of the hillside, trickling between mossy boulders and funnelling its way into a pipe. But it did not feel right and he did not think that was what the Garuda meant. Suddenly, without any effort on his part, or perhaps in spite of his imaginings, the brilliant blue was transformed, and Jigme could see quite vividly a stone wall with a carved head projecting out of it.

It was the head of a strange beast with its snout curled back, round eyes and flattened ears. Its jaws were wide open and water was flowing out of its mouth in a steady stream. The scene was bathed in a pale, bluish light and Jigme noticed how clear and clean the water looked and how small, bright green ferns had lodged themselves in the stonework.

There seemed to be an immense amount of warbling and clucking going on around him, but he had no desire to open his eyes and see what the birds were doing. The dream-like vision was beginning to absorb him completely. He had noticed a very slender, emerald-coloured snake was easing its way along the head of the water-spout. Another mushroom-brown one was rearing up from below, its forked tongue flicking at the water as it fell.

Louder and shriller grew the bird sounds, as if they were trying to distract him. Jigme was tempted to cover his ears, but he would have had to summon an extraordinary amount of will-power to move his hands from his knees. He was hypnotised by the scene unfolding before him. The small green serpent had reached the end of the water-spout and was turning its tiny diamond-shaped head towards him.

Just as it fixed its brilliant, glittering eyes in his direction, all the individual screechings and cawings blended and rose together into a single, ear-splitting note. There was a blinding flash of light and what felt like a powerful explosion. Immediately Jigme found himself in pitch darkness with his head ringing as if he had been struck rather hard from behind.

Alarmed and full of apprehension, he opened his eyes to see what had happened. As a million points of light danced in front of him he wondered if perhaps he was dead. Then as they settled into a uniform greyish-blue it occurred to him that perhaps he was really looking at the sky.

Becoming conscious of his body again he found he was lying rather uncomfortably on his back, with his legs still crossed and his knees sticking up in the air. Something hard and lumpy was sticking in his back.

Cautiously he looked sideways and found he was lying in a furrow between two ridges of earth. Leafy plants were growing on them. On close inspection – which required no movement whatsoever as they were only a few inches from his nose – he saw quite clearly that they were potatoes.

He struggled upright and looked around. He was in the middle of a small, cultivated field, bordered by thorny hedges. A couple of dozen yards in front of him was a low, stone wall with a few ancient-looking trees nearby. He found his bag lying on the mound to his left, half-concealed among the potato plants. His hat was still on his head.

He got to his feet a little unsteadily and brushed the dirt from his clothes. He seemed to be back in the valley again. It was late afternoon. The sun was already behind the hills, but there was still daylight left. A cuckoo was calling to its mate and somewhere in the distance a goat was bleating.

Feeling slightly giddy, Jigme approached the wall with the idea of sitting on it for a moment to collect himself. He could see a muddy trail running along the edge of the field and a few red-tiled farmhouses not far away. Smoke from a bonfire was drifting along the top of the hedgerow and rising violet and yellow into the late afternoon sky.

He reached the wall and looked over. It contained, not another vegetable garden as he had imagined, but a sunken, stone courtyard. There was a short flight of steps on one side leading down to a washing place. Leaning over a little further he could see directly underneath him was a carved water-spout, with water spilling out in a steady stream and splashing onto the paving below. From the angle he was at it was not completely visible, but he knew without any doubt it was the spout he had seen in his vision.

He made his way round to the head of the steps. From this side he could see the round, bulbous eyes and the trunk-like upper lip curled back from the beast's open mouth. The place seemed empty and abandoned. Jigme descended into the courtyard. Pushing back his sleeves he cupped the cold water in his hands and splashed it on his face. It felt so good that he did it several times, allowing it to run down his eyelids and trickle over his cheeks.

When at last he wiped himself dry with his sleeve and looked up he was no longer alone. A slim, green snake with tiny black eyes had anchored itself to the water-spout with its tail and was leaning down to scrutinise him.

Several things went through Jigme's mind very fast.

"Sometimes tiny snakes are the most deadly."

"This is the one I saw right at the beginning."

"I wonder if my hat's on straight."

The last thought prompted him to feel for the feathers on his cap. What had the Garuda said? He must remember it was his ceremonial crown. Jigme tucked in his chin and tried to hold his head erect. Beyond the music of the water falling on the flagstones he could hear rustlings and raspings and other softer, silky sounds. They were coming from all around him. He turned slowly.

Small and large, hanging and slithering, the courtyard had been taken over by snakes. In their midst, three-and-a-half times coiled on a wide stone shelf sat one so large its presence dominated all the rest. It was black with red eyes and an enormous cobra-like hood. On top of its head sat another tiny, white snake, shining and translucent as if it rarely saw the light of day.

Jigme's instinctive reaction was to run for his life. He might well have done so had a long, sinewy diamond-back not draped itself over the steps. Perhaps it was not purposely blocking his way out, but Jigme was not inclined to risk a head-on encounter with it. He tried to keep a grip on himself.

The huge, black serpent, which he could only assume was the Naga King, was eying him speculatively.

"You wear some fancy feathers in your hat," it breathed, swaying threateningly close and flicking its forked tongue this way and that. "Are they just for show or are you really fearlessss?"

The tiny white snake on his hood hissed in merriment.

Jigme swallowed hard. His mouth felt very dry.

"Well...." Jigme faltered. He was not sure if he should address the naga as an equal. He was, after all, supposed to be representing the Garuda. After a moment's hesitation he decided to settle for respect rather than risk insulting such a powerful creature. "Well, Your Highness, you see my mother's very sick and I was told you might be able to help me. I'm trying to find a cure for her."

"I ssseee," said the naga.

Then there was a long silence. The naga swayed from side to side, its gaze fixed on Jigme unwaveringly. The boy thought it quite possible it might dart forward at any moment and bite him. He felt as if those glinting, red eyes were trying to hypnotise him. He had heard of snakes mesmerising their victims before striking them down.

Indeed Jigme might well have also fallen into a trance were it not for the fact that a very inquisitive, smaller snake had wound itself round his leg and was investigating the inside of his felt boot. He wanted desperately to relieve the tickling sensation by scratching the back of his knee.

"Yessss," said the snake at last, his sibilant voice just audible above the sound of splashing from the spout. "The human being is a mindless creature. It makes the waters upstream filthy and the people downstream sick. It cuts the forests down and cries for rain. It carves up the earth hunting for riches and wonders why its own kind suffers from famine and disease. Sssuch ignorance!"

A couple of other snakes who had slipped their way over the stones to listen bobbed their heads in agreement and hissed softly.

"Yessss, most regrettable."

The Nagaraj continued to stare at Jigme in its intense and discomfiting fashion.

"There are of course a few of you who manage to redeem the human race somewhat, otherwise there wouldn't be much point in your existence I wouldn't think."

The naga flipped the tip of his shiny, black tail to and fro as if in mild irritation.

"Fortunately for you, I am bound by oath to your mother's family. The Great Lord Garuda went to a lot of unnecessary trouble to protect you. Though perhaps it was just as well. If you had irked me I might have forgotten myself and felt like teaching you an impromptu lesson."

His forked tongue whipped this way and that as if reaching for invisible delicacies.

Jigme decided this was perhaps the moment to offer his silk scarf and ensure the serpent's continuing good will. He took it from his pocket and, unfolding it carefully, presented it on his outstretched palms. The Nagaraj stared at it for a moment and then slowly lowered his head. Jigme leaned forward and, avoiding the little, white snake as best he could, placed it over the naga's hood. The naga straightened himself up again, the scarf hanging gracefully on either side of its head, and although its expression had not changed at all, its attitude seemed to the boy a little less threatening.

Boy and serpent looked at each other; one with grave attention, wondering what would happen next, the other with a glittering fiery gaze that betrayed nothing.

"Come closer and stand at ease," said the Naga King at last in a whispering hiss."I have a story to tell you, if you have the patience to listen."

Jigme inched forward a little, taking care not to trample any of the snakes around his feet.

"Yessss. That's better."

The naga bobbed its head a little lower.

"Now I shall begin. Long ago in the olden days, when your many times great-grandmother was a girl, the King of this valley arranged a marriage between his daughter and the young King of the Northern Plateau. It was a time when the people recognised our power to protect against sickness and ill-fortune. Yessss! Even the poorest people had the sense to make ritual offerings of milk and incense to us nagas on certain days of the year. No one would have dreamed of dirtying the springs or polluting the rivers. Everyone knew pure drinking water was far too important for life."

"In return it was not uncommon for a member of the White Naga family to make its home wherever devout humans kept their wealth, and guard it against thieves and robbers. One such snake – a cousin of mine – whose name was Motiraj Naga, lived in the palace treasury. He was well fed and highly respected and spent his days coiled happily among the gold and jewellery of the royal household. He was a naga of some considerable power, but was very small in size."

"It was time for the King's daughter to go and join her future husband. The King, as it was the custom in those days of course, was offering a suitably regal dowry for his daughter's marriage, and when the royal treasurer went to gather up some gems and ornaments for it from the palace vaults, he unwittingly scooped little Motiraj into the wedding chest with them and trapped him inside."

"The journey up over the mountains took the bridal procession several weeks on horseback. All the while my cousin Motiraj was locked in the jewel box, bumping along on the backs of pack animals, dizzy and confused by this turn of events."

"Eventually the princess and her entourage arrived at their destination, and all the trunks and boxes were unloaded. The dowry chest was transported into the King's chamber and the royal household gathered round to see what wonderful things the Princess had brought, for the Valley Kingdom has always been famous for the unrivalled skill of its gold and silversmiths. The copper bands sealing the trunk were removed, the straps unbuckled and the lid flung back."

"Yessss! A splendid vision of ruby necklaces and carved golden bracelets met their eyes. There were wonderful statues and ornate drinking vessels, pearl necklaces and a special ring for the King with nine precious gems to ensure him lifelong protection from the planets. He couldn't have been more satisfied."

"Motiraj, buried in the midst of this treasure, smelled fresh air at last and wriggled his way up to the surface. We must forgive these ignorant people from the North, I suppose, for they had never before seen such a ghostly, pale naga in their rough and inhospitable realms. They were struck instantly by irrational terror."

"The princess herself, tired from her long journey, had withdrawn to her new quarters to rest, otherwise she could have told them at once who Motiraj was. As it was pandemonium broke out. Ah! What foolishness. The general opinion was that this intruder was a foreign devil of some kind, and the King's attendants leapt forward on the attack with daggers and fire tongs and anything else they could lay their hands on."

"Cousin Motiraj, weakened by weeks of deprivation, kept up a dignified defence as long as he could, but eventually, caught at an angle by a blow from a soup ladle, he was swept out of the chest, through the air and into the shadowy recesses of the room, where a servant girl was standing. This girl was in fact the greatest of your great-grandmothers, and when she saw this tiny, white cobra land at her feet she felt terribly sorry for him. He looked to her no more than a baby."

"The rest of the household scrambled over the furniture, up-turning tables and tossing aside cushions in a vain attempt to find where he had gone. Such fools they were! But your ancestor, being a compulsive girl with a good heart, quickly took a copper tea-urn off the shelf. She removed the lid and, laying the pot down on floor level, tapped on the bottom and whispered:

""Jump in!""

"Seeing a protective-looking, black hole in front of him, our naga didn't need telling twice, and with a quick flip of the tail he was inside the teapot. Gently putting the lid back on, the girl stood up and bearing the pot before her casually, as if on the way to the kitchen, left the room. Once the door was closed behind her, she ran downstairs to her room and stuffed the pot under her bed. Then fearing her presence would be missed she went back to join the chaos in the royal chamber."

"Though he could easily have escaped out of the spout, Motiraj decided his best plan was to stay put. For the rest of the day he lay curled in the bottom of the copper urn to see what would happen next. He wasn't afraid. We nagas are never afraid. But he had no intention of laying himself victim to those clumsy barbarians again."

"At nightfall your greatest great-ancestor came back to her room and pulled the pot out from under the bed. She had had plenty of time for second and third thoughts about her action. She knew she would have to return the pot soon, before someone accused her of stealing it, but she really didn't know what to do with the strange, little creature inside it. She had become a little nervous about it all. Still, thinking Motiraj might be hungry she had brought him a small bowl of butter tea, which she laid on the floorboards in front of the pot."

"Attracted by the steamy smell, my cousin wriggled his way out, slid down the handle and, desperate for nourishment after his long fast, approached the bowl. He found the tea quite horrible. It seemed to have been made with butter that was very old, if not quite rancid. It was not at all to the taste of a royal serpent who was used to fresh cow's milk. However, if he was to survive he needed sustenance, and the girl, while knowing nothing about anything, was at least trying to save his life. So he drank as much of the dreadful liquid as he could."

"As she knelt on the wooden floor, your great-grand-ancestor watched with fascination. She had never before seen anything so pale and pearly-white as Motiraj. He looked to her like a magical, moonstone necklace that had come to life. She would have liked to keep him forever. But she understood he didn't belong in her land of harsh winds and month-long snows. He looked too naked and exotic, and she knew she would have to devise a way to get him back to the Princess' homeland."

"The wedding was celebrated with much drinking and dancing that went on for days. The noise alone gave Motiraj a headache. He lived in an old brass and wood beer pot on the girl's windowsill. Slightly disgusted by his reduced circumstances he was grateful nevertheless for his daily diet of yak-butter tea."

"Then one morning when the first bitter winds of winter made themselves felt around the palace, the soldiers that had accompanied the princess as an escort on her journey made ready to return to the sacred, green valley."

"As a friendly gesture to his new father and mother-in-law, the King of the Northern Plateau prepared a bundle of precious silks from China to be sent with the soldiers as a gift. Seeing her chance, your greater-than-great-grandmother hid Motiraj in her sleeve. Then, making a show of helping to pack the silk into the leather saddlebags, she furtively slipped the naga in with the fabrics, making sure he slid well down to the bottom and wouldn't fall out. When no one was watching she bent and whispered good luck to him, tied up the thongs on the bag flaps, and before long he was on his way home."

"Weeks later when the courtiers in the valley palace unrolled the fabulous silks for the king and queen to see, they were all so enraptured by the folds of shimmering pinks and blues that nobody noticed Motiraj. He slipped away quietly to the royal treasury, squeezed under the door and was back in his familiar haunt once more. There was even a bowl of milk waiting for him, left that morning by the king's priest."

The King of the Nagas paused in reflection and breathed a hissing sigh.

"Knowing how we serpents feel about these things, I suspect he felt more than a little offended that no one seemed to have even noticed his absence. On the other hand some might say the priest's continued devotion helped to ensure Motiraj's safe return. Who can tell?"

"What I do remember my cousin saying was that, surprisingly, the cow's milk didn't taste nearly as good on his return as he had thought it would. In fact he had acquired quite a taste for yak butter tea instead. But then as the weeks passed by everything returned to normal. He lived peacefully among the gold and the gemstones once more, guarding the royal treasure from the wicked and greedy. If truth be known he still does to this day."

The snake tested the air with the tips of his tongue a few times.

"There was of course a point to this story. Do you ssssee?"

He dipped his head so that his red, glowing eyes were on a level with Jigme's. It was quite an experience and fortunately the boy was not expected to provide an answer.

"Yessss! Your family and mine have a bond. As you are directly descended from the girl who saved my cousin's life, I am duty bound to help you when you need my assistance."

The Nagaraj reared up into a regal posture once more.

"Your mother's sickness will not last long. Strangers passing through your village were careless of your customs and left their bad dreams behind. She was caught unawares by them as the season changed and was chilled by unhealthy waters."

"I shall give you a gift. It is of great value if you know how to use it. Remember to keep it safely and it will serve you and your family well."

The great serpent narrowed his eyes and gave a little shudder that travelled down his back, round and round his black coils and ended by disappearing at the tip of his tail. Then he began to tremble. As his whole body shook he seemed to have a series of convulsions. A strange noise issued from his throat.

"Gup-a-gup-a-gup."

And suddenly a bright, ruby-coloured stone appeared in his mouth.

"Quick! Quick, catch it!" squealed the small white snake.

At the same moment that Jigme put out his hand, the Nagaraj spat and the gem fell into his outstretched palm. It felt strangely cool against Jigme's skin and gave off a deep reddish glow in the fading daylight. A dozen voices began to hiss at him. Reaching up on the very tip of her tail a female serpent whispered in his ear.

"Go quickly! Don't waste a moment! He might change his mind."

The diamond-back on the stone staircase slithered encouragingly to the side to make way and Jigme decided to take the advice to heart. Holding the stone tightly between thumb and forefinger he bowed respectfully to the Naga King and hurried up out of the courtyard.

When he reached the wall at the top he turned for one quick look back. He paused and blinked. The courtyard was completely deserted. In the deepening twilight there was nothing to be seen but the falling stream of water, which rang out as it struck the empty paving stones.

It was late and dark by the time Jigme reached Bhote Bazaar once more. He had no difficulty in finding the truck driver and his friends. Or rather they had no difficulty in spotting him as he walked up the street. They greeted him warmly.

"Hey, little tiger boy, where've you been?"

"We thought we'd lost you."

"Did you find what you were looking for?"

"Oh man, look at him, he's asleep on his feet."

It was true. He was completely exhausted and no sooner had they shown him where he could lie down than he collapsed in a deep and motionless slumber.

The next day they set off before it was light and were soon climbing out of the warm green valley again. Up they went into the chill, damp mists that separated the lowlands from the high plateau to the North. The truck was not quite so comfortable to sit in this time. The huge bundles of wool had been replaced by grain sacks and wooden crates, but Jigme hardly noticed. He perched near the tailboard watching as the lush cultivated fields vanished behind them and the world was enveloped in clouds of fog.

As it grew colder he buttoned his coat and put on his hat, but not before he had extracted the Garuda feathers and put them away safely. Every so often he felt for the little, wooden dagger at his throat and the naga-stone knotted into his shirt, just to reassure himself that they really existed. If not for these tangible proofs he felt he might have dreamed the last few days.

And so the miles passed and the hours passed. When the truck stopped for the night he slept rolled in a sheepskin, squeezed in between the wooden boxes. In the daytime he sang and yawned and dozed, perched on top of them. The driver had told him they were taking a road that would pass not too far from the way to his village. He promised to stop there and shout when it was time for Jigme to get down.

It was the morning of the third day and Jigme had been lulled into sleep by the endless motion when something terrible happened. The truck hit a particularly large pothole, the pin securing the tailboard leapt in its socket and the back of the truck flew open. In a moment Jigme was tossed off his box like a bundle of rubbish and hit the road with a sickening bump. Shocked and confused he opened his eyes just in time to see the vehicle through clouds of billowing dust disappearing without him. He was completely stunned. For a few minutes it was impossible for him to understand how to get to his feet, let alone run after the truck. All he could manage to do was to sit up and bleat pathetically.

"Stop! Stop! You're going without me."

Then he lay back and tried to feel if he was badly hurt or not. He twitched his toes, lifted his knees, stretched his arms and fingered the back of his head. It was already beginning to grow a large lump but his thick woollen hat had protected him from anything worse. He stayed prone in the dirt, feeling sick and dismayed, not wishing to think about the seriousness of his predicament.

"Ow! Ow! Ow! Ow! Ow!"

What on earth was that? It was a noise of pain and misery that might have been his own if he had not been perfectly sure he had not uttered so much as a squeak. He blinked and listened carefully.

"Oooooh! Ow! Ow! Ow!"

He felt so shaken and sore he did not want to move at all, but curiosity was prodding him and he raised his head cautiously to look around. It was a painful undertaking, but he was met with a sight so unexpected that for a moment he experienced nothing but astonishment. An old woman was sitting by the side of the road with what looked like his shoulder bag on her head.

"Ooooh! That hurts. It hurts all over. Ow! Ow! Ow!"

Jigme felt quite annoyed. He was the one who hurt all over. What was she making such a noise for? And what was she doing with his bag? He levered himself up on one elbow. She did not seem to see him however, her eyes were screwed up and great tears were rolling down her cheeks.

He flopped back into his dip in the road and closed his eyes. She went on crying.

"Ooooh! I feel so sore. My poor old back. Ow!"

The distressing noise continued unabated until Jigme felt impelled to do something. He was tempted to shout at her to be quiet, but it occurred to him that perhaps she might have been hit by the truck at the same moment that he fell out of it. He blew the dust out of his nostrils and sat up a little shakily. He took another look. She did not seem to be hurt, and she looked very peculiar wearing his bag as a hat.

The more she howled, the less his own body seemed to be in pain. He had never seen a grown up crying quite like this. She was sobbing like an infant. He struggled to collect himself and went to sit beside her on the grass verge.

"What's the matter?' he asked.

"What do you mean "what's the matter"?" she retorted in a voice thick with grief and her nose pouring tears and mucous. "Can't you see?"

Jigme wondered what she meant.

"Look at me! I used to be so beautiful. I used to be the best dancer in the village. All the men wanted to make love to me and look at me now! Look at my hands they look like badly cured goat skin. Look at my face! The flesh is all falling off."

She plucked at a fold on her cheek.

"I hurt all over and I'm so ugly!"

Jigme was a little frightened by the force of her revulsion and pulled his coat around him for protection. She still had not looked at him. His fingers felt instinctively for the naga-stone tied in the end of his shirt, and finding its smooth coolness reassuring even through a layer of cloth, he held it firmly in the palm of his left hand hidden underneath the coat flap.

He did not know what he was supposed to say. It was true, she did look rather hideous. But then that was because she was a picture of self-pity and misery with her eyes screwed up and her drooling mouth. Her peculiar piece of headwear did not help.

"Please could I have my bag back?"

"Your bag? What bag?"

Jigme hesitated a little.

"The one on your head."

The old woman snatched it off and peered at it in disbelief.

"Ow! Ow! Ow! Ow!"

She flung it in Jigme's direction and covered her eyes with her fists.

"I used to be the most stylishly dressed woman in town. All the ladies tried to copy me. I used to be so clever. And look at me now. Dressed in rags and dressed in bags. I'm losing my mind as well."

Her words were drowned once more as she was convulsed by howls and sobs.

""What happened to my turquoise hair ornaments? Why is my skin all rough and crinkled? Where did these lumps on my feet come from?"

She seemed so disgusted by her condition that Jigme was beginning to be disgusted by her too. As a wave of nausea washed over him, he noticed there was a strange sensation in his hand. A peculiar prickling feeling like pins and needles seemed to be radiating from the naga's jewel where it sat cupped in his palm.

"It used to be all black and shiny," the old woman was tugging at her grizzled, grey plaits, "and so long that I could sit on it. Now it's just like bits of string."

Then she let out a terrible lonely wail.

"I want my mother. Oh, Ma! Oh, Ma!"

There was something both comical and tragic about the old woman's behaviour. If Jigme had had a friend or ally to hand, he probably would have had no choice but to succumb to an attack of the giggles, but as it was he felt acutely uncomfortable. He was not at all sure what to do. There was also the extraordinary sensation he was experiencing, as if the jewel was shining in his hand, although he could not see it hidden underneath his coat.

"I wish I knew how to help her," he thought.

At once the woman looked at him for the first time, narrowing her swollen eyes as if to assess what kind of a creature he was. She sniffed and wiped her cheeks.

"I can tell you how to help me," she said eagerly. "Just give me that snake's jewel you have concealed in your shirt."

"I should have guessed," thought Jigme. "She's some kind of a witch. What do I do now?"

He turned away from her and gazed back down the dusty road. He really did not want to give the jewel away. He wanted to keep it for his mother and himself. He felt he had earned it. He got to his feet and wandered a few yards down the road scuffing the stony dirt with his boots. His head throbbed and the bump on the back of it had grown to the size of a small apricot. The old woman was silent now and sat watching him hopefully.

The jewel seemed to be spitting fiery darts through the material of his shirt and into the flesh of his fingers. He thought of all the wise and helpful people he had encountered since he left home, not to mention the strange birds and beasts. He wondered what they would expect of him.

"I wish I knew what to do," he sighed inwardly.

Suddenly the tune the magician of the island had sung began playing in his head, along with a song which was coming fully formed into his mind. Before he knew what he was doing, he was singing it out loud:

"The lama told me nothing lasts,
It's foolish to hang on;
A bubble on the water
Stays a moment, then its gone.

The wizard said each creature
Needs my help because you know
It could have been my mother
In a lifetime long ago.

The cliff-top baba said "Beware,
Don't judge things in advance."
His cousin said "Relax your mind!"
And showed me how to dance.

I learned to make a bow
And how to shoot an arrow straight.
The lovely, wise yogini said
"Be kind and concentrate."

Garuda said "Keep balanced
Hold your back straight and stay calm."
The Naga King coughed up a jewel
And spat it in my palm.

A granny sitting by the road
Was desperate she said.
As I was wondering what to do
A voice spoke in my head.

"Offer your wish-fulfilling gem
To those who have the least.
You never know what you'll be next
A man, or ghost, or beast,
You never know what you'll be next
A man, or ghost, or beast!"

On the final note Jigme twirled around with a flourish and began untying the knot in his shirt.

"Alright you can have it," he said to the old woman.

Swiftly he slipped the Nagaraja's jewel into his hand and held it out to her before a clever, contrary, little voice inside might try to make him change his mind.

"Here."

The old woman got to her feet and peered into his palm. Jigme gazed down at the stone too. It lay there, cool and still once more, shimmering faintly with a ruby lustre. It looked very beautiful to his eyes. There was silence for a moment and then the old woman sniffed disappointedly.

"Poof! What's that dingy old pebble? That's not what I'm looking for at all. Ah me, how unsettling. I thought you had the wishing jewel, but I was wrong. How very unsettling."

The boy watched her in astonishment. She shook the dust from her clothes. Wiped her eyes with the corner of her apron and smoothed her hair.

"Another day maybe," she whispered to herself.

Then she wagged a wrinkled finger under Jigme's nose.

"You don't want to go believing everything you're told, you know. That thing's not a real naga-stone. It'll never make any of your wishes come true, no matter how hard you try. Ha!"

She stared at him for a moment.

"Still, it's a good thing you came along. There's no point in me making a fool of myself shedding useless tears. You reminded me my grandson's waiting for his lunch. He likes greens in his soup. Now, didn't I have a hat with me?"

She ran her hand uncertainly over the top of her head.

"Ah, maybe not. Dear, dear. Talk about making something out of nothing. Alright I'm going now," and she waddled off away from the road in the direction of some distant houses.

Jigme stared blankly after her, his hand still held out in front of him. His mind felt quite weak and befuddled and for a while he could not take his eyes off her hunched back retreating across the dusty fields. Then the spell was broken and the giggle that had been trying to get out for quite some time erupted from his stomach in a kind of chirrup. It was followed swiftly by a couple more and then he was shaking all over with laughter. Taking a last look at the rosy, oval stone in his palm, he knotted it into the bottom of his shirt once more and tucked it away under his coat.

"You never know what you'll be next....."

He had had neither the time to try and make sense of what had happened, nor to consider what he ought to do next now that he was lost in the middle of nowhere, when he heard the sound of an approaching motor horn. Shortly afterwards his friends reappeared, roaring over the hill towards him in their familiar truck. They stopped beside him in a cloud of dust.

The driver craned his neck out of the window, hawked and spat and looked Jigme over.

"Well, there he is! I'm not sure why he's grinning like a monkey, but there he is!"

The driver's partner pushed his head out too.

"Looks like he's in one piece. Hey, man, you gave us quite a fright. We stopped to take a leisurely lunch and three crates, the bedding roll and tiger-boy had vanished. You okay?"

Jigme nodded. He could tell it was true; he was still grinning from ear to ear and did not know how to stop.

"Maybe he's had a crack on the head and it's knocked him silly. Here. You'd better come and sit up front."

He opened the cab and hauled Jigme in.

"We can't afford to have you flying out a second time!"

It was only an hour or two later that the road came in sight of the great river. The driver kindly took a small detour to get Jigme as close to it as he could without getting the truck wheels stuck in the dunes and the boy clambered out. He said good-bye to his friends, feeling sure he would meet them again some time in the future, and as the lorry turned and began lumbering away eastwards, he waved to them until they were no longer visible. Then he climbed to the top of a high sandbank to get his bearings.

The water margin was hidden from where he stood, but he could see quite clearly, some way downstream among the cliffs and spurs that bordered his side of the river, one with familiar carved white rocks. It was the landmark his uncle had told him to look for on his way to visit the lama. That meant he was very close to the ferry landing. It had to be somewhere between the white rocks and where he was standing.

He had been bumping over the road with his knees up for so many days that it felt good to use his legs, and the cool air coming up from the water was invigourating. He bounded his way up and down sandy ridges and over rocky outcroppings, long dry tufts of grass whisking at his legs as he went. Then, even before he expected it, he rounded a twist in the bank and he was in sight of the ferry. And it was just pushing off from shore.

Jigme ran across the muddy flat towards the river's edge.

"Wait for me! Please wait for me!" he shouted.

The ferryman turned steadying the boat with his pole.

"Woah! Look who's here! It's our young friend the goat tamer. You're just in time. Jump in! Here catch this."

As Jigme scrambled aboard, the boatman flung the rope at him and pushed the craft out of the shallows and into the current. Then the motor roared into life.

This time Jigme had a chance to enjoy the beauty of the great river. He sprawled on a narrow plank that spanned the ferry as a makeshift seat, and dangling his fingers in the water, he watched the sky overhead. The wind had changed and the clouds made a strange, dappled pattern, like fish scales, white against the blue.

"Not dragon's breath but dragon's skin", he thought.

It was doubly reflected in the ripples on the surface of the glistening water and flecked the wood of the boat with splashes of light.

"I'm floating down the river to meet my love.
Her lips are coral and her skin is white.
She's free as a falcon in the sky above.
Her eyes are the stars of night.

I'll be one with her, she'll be one with me,
My turquoise lady with the rainbow heart,
When the river meets the waters of the open sea
Never again to part.

I'm floating down the river to meet my love,
Never again to part."

The ferryman's melodious, husky voice rose above the chugging of the engine and carried them safely through the dangerous eddies and around the sandbanks until they finally reached the other side.

Jigme pulled off his boots and waded to the bank with the rope. The water was shockingly cold and very pleasurable to his dusty feet. He was suddenly excited to be on his home shore and impatient to reach his village. He felt he had had quite enough of travelling.

Half-an-hour up the road Jigme was overtaken by a tractor with a trailer full of oil cans. It was going very slowly but it was still faster than being on foot and when the driver offered him a lift to a hamlet not too far from his home village, Jigme happily climbed on the back.

The motor made a terrible noise, scaring every pika and marmot for miles, and it was so bumpy Jigme's teeth felt as if they were in danger of being rattled out of their sockets. The river receded behind them and soon Jigme began to recognise the familiar landmarks of the fields and hills he had known all his life.

After running alongside several huge barley fields they came to a cluster of houses where the driver brought his tractor to a halt. Jigme's village was in sight and the boy jumped down from the trailer and set off in the direction of home.

He was still a couple of hundred yards from the first outlying farmhouses when a small figure came hurtling down the road to greet him. It was Leo. The little dog jumped up at him and circled him with his tail wagging, making playful growls and squeals that seemed to be both noises of delight at his return and reprimands for his absence. Jigme could not help wondering how the small dog had known he was coming, and if he had been sitting somewhere on the outskirts of the village on look-out ever since his departure.

Pleased to be in each other's company once more they passed through the gateway into the village and turned down the street to Jigme's house. It was nearly dusk and a fine haze of smoke from the first evening fires hung over the rooftops.

Someone was standing on the doorstep of Jigme's house and gave a friendly wave. As they got nearer Jigme realised with surprise that it was Yongden, his eldest brother. He had not expected to see him for some time.

"Hi there!"

"Hi"

"The wanderer returns!" said Yongden with a smile and punched him affectionately in the chest.

"What are you doing back?" asked Jigme. "Why aren't you up in the high pastures looking after the animals?"

"The weather's changed. There's going to be some late snow up there. Dad thought it would be a good idea if I brought the cheese and butter down to market early. Then I can take some things we need back up tomorrow before the trail gets difficult. But how was your trip? Where did you spend the night?"

"Which night?"

"Last night of course," said Yongden, looking at him a little oddly.

"Oh, across the river," answered Jigme being purposely vague, although he could not have explained why. Then, not wishing his brother to think he was being secretive he added "I'll tell you about it later. How's Mum?"

"She's much better today. You should go tell her you're back. She's in the kitchen."

The house was full of the smell of his mother's cooking, which reminded him of crossing the poisoned lake and made him want to laugh. He experienced a moment of giddy weightlessness as if all the experiences of the past week were condensing very fast into the present moment and time and space had no meaning any more.

His mother was standing by the stove with her back to him. Her arms were raised as she pinned back one of her braids that had come loose. The silky material of her blouse fell to her elbows in folds, revealing her conch-shell bracelets. Her keys hung glinting from her belt.

Very, very quietly Jigme crept up behind her holding his breath. Carefully he took hold of the keys so they would not clink against each other. Then, slowly and silently he tried to see if he could unhook them.

Of course he did not stand a chance. She spun round and pounced on him at once. Then, discovering it was only Jigme trying to trick her, she gave him a hug.

"Well, my cunning little son, if you want to grow up to be a fox or a pick-pocket, you'll have to do better than that! But you did give me a fright."

She let him go and straightened up to take a better look at him.

"I had a wonderful dream of you last night. You offered me milk in a lapiz bowl and it tasted of every delicious thing I could possibly imagine. It ran through all the veins in my body until I felt like flying. And then when I woke this morning I was so much better I didn't need to take the medicine any more."

She smiled.

"Go and tell your brother the food's ready. We can eat early. You're probably hungry."

And so the three of them sat down to a dinner of meat dumplings with hot sauce. They were made the way his mother always made them – neat and round and fluted on top, with not too much pastry dough and not too little either. Jigme did not count how many he had, but he ate and ate until he could hardly move.

When at last the bowls had been cleared away and they were sitting back in comfort, Yongden turned to his little brother once more.

"Well now you're full and the evening's only just begun you can tell us about your trip. I'm really curious."

"Yes so am I," said his mother. "What happened? Did you have any adventures? Where did you go to?"

So Jigme began to tell his story, starting with great-uncle Rabten's advice, then the goat and the ferryman, and on to his visit with the great lama.

While he was talking the next-door-neighbour dropped in to borrow their carpet-wool clippers and was so taken with Jigme's story that he sat down to listen instead. After a little his daughter came by to see what had happened to him and she sat down too.

Jigme told them of the lynx on the mountain and the poisoned lake, the talking frog and the magician on the island, and as he talked the lady from across the road came in, so did the boy from the village bakery and the bootmaker and his sister until the room was quite crowded.

Before long the congenial atmosphere and warmth attracted a pair of street dogs. When no one was watching they stole in and made themselves comfortable under a table and at some point a passing beggar wandered in too and settled close to the stove. Nobody noticed just when he joined the audience, but after a while he was unarguably there, sniffing and scratching himself and laughing with pleasure at the story.

Somebody brought in a kettle full of tea and somebody else passed round sweets and barley crackers. Noises from the street fell away and the silence of the night enveloped the village. No one interrupted Jigme. No one wanted to leave before the story was over and it was not until quite late in the evening that he was finally describing his boat ride back across the river and the tractor that picked him up just when he was beginning to wish the journey was at an end.

"Then as I turned down our street I saw Yongden on the doorstep and I was back home again...."

Jigme turned and smiled at his brother.

"...and that's it," he said and slumped back in his seat exhausted.

There was a moment of complete silence before everyone started talking at once, applauding and laughing and shaking their heads in disbelief.

"Well done!"

"What a story!"

"How did you manage that I wonder?"

"How very curious."

"I'd planned to do so many things at home this evening but I just couldn't tear myself away."

"Imagine going all the way down to the green, southern valley and back!"

Yongden leaned over and gently pulled Jigme by the ear.

"Little brother, you're extraordinary. If you can make up stories like that at the twitch of a yak's tail you should come up to the high pastures and keep us entertained in the long evenings. If I didn't know you'd only been gone overnight I might even have believed it all!"

Jigme felt a strange dizziness coming over him. What did his brother mean? It made no sense. He slipped his hand under his outer clothing and felt for the naga-stone. His fingers encountered nothing but the soft fabric of his shirt. His stomach plunged and for a moment a chilly vortex seemed about to engulf him.

He sat up and made his back as straight as he could. He tried to keep his anxiety at bay and explored the seams of his shirt more carefully. The room was emptying out. The friends and neighbours made their way home. There was the sound of heavy doors being bolted, voices dying away in the distance and sporadic barking before the still and empty night settled around the house once more. The beggar sat hunched in his spot beside the stove. He was almost sure that Jigme's mother would not turn him out of doors at this late hour, but he was nevertheless trying to make himself unobtrusive. Leo was sleeping on the cushion next to Jigme's. His paws twitched from time to time and he uttered brief, muffled whimpers as if dreams of a chase transported him through a different world.

Jigme's fingers encountered an oval lump in the small of his back and recognised the cool smoothness of the naga-stone beneath the twisted cloth of his shirt tail. A wave of relief swept over him, but it was not enough to dispel his bewilderment.

He watched his mother collecting up the tea things and straightening out the rugs.

"How long was I gone?" he asked.

She paused with the white and blue dragon bowl in her hands – the one she kept for special guests – and looked at him with her head tilted a little to the side.

"Well, I woke at dawn and you were already gone, so I can't say exactly. It depends how many hours you were walking in the dark."

She turned to the beggar and set the bowl and a pair of chopsticks gently down in front of him.

"Here, there's just one helping of dumplings left. You eat them and I'll get you a blanket."

Jigme stared at the bowl as the beggar picked it up. A fine spiral of steam rose from it and vanished. Perhaps the painted, blue flames on it flickered a little but he was growing too drowsy to be sure. He lay down among the cushions and watched the beggar sideways.

With gnarled and grimy fingers the old man raised his chop sticks and skillfully plucked a portion of dumpling from the bowl. He balanced it with care on the lid of the kettle beside him, murmuring a few inaudible words as he did so. There was a flurry of movement accompanied by squeaks and titters and a purring of wings. Then, as if several greedy but invisible mouths were devouring it between them, the morsel of food broke into several pieces and disappeared.

The old beggar looked over at Jigme and winked at him. He seemed extraordinarily familiar. Jigme gazed at him, puzzled by the dawning realisation that he was not a stranger but someone Jigme knew very well indeed. He wanted to look more closely and identify those curled eyebrows and the slightly crooked mouth that twitched with concealed laughter. He was sure that if only he could stretch his mind one step more beyond its present horizon he would remember who the beggar was and how he had met him.

But the blue, painted dragons on the porcelain bowl were distracting him. Without any doubt at all they had begun to weave their way among the azure flames, and, try as he might, the effort of doing anything other than watch in fascination was more than he could manage. Their sapphire scales glimmered against the pearly glaze. The lapiz fire flickered. Then lifting off with a serpentine wriggle, they began to glide upwards and melt into a coil of opalescent mist. As the night folded over him he slept, with the naga-stone still clasped securely in his hand.

THE END

117

This book is dedicated to the memory of my
beloved and fearless teachers:
Terry Frost, Chogyam Trungpa Rinpoche,
Gangotri Baba, Dilgo Khyentse Rinpoche and
Chogye Trichen Rinpoche.